Terri Blackstock

AUTHOR

Downfall

TITLE

DATE DUE	BORROWER'S NAME

DOWNFALL

TERRI BLACKSTOCK

THORNDIKE PRESS

A part of Gale, Cengage Learning

GALE
CENGAGE Learning·

Detroit • New York • San Francisco • New Haven, Conn • Waterville, Maine • London

GALE
CENGAGE Learning®

Copyright © 2012 by Terri Blackstock.
Thorndike Press, a part of Gale, Cengage Learning.

ALL RIGHTS RESERVED
Any internet addresses (websites, blogs, etc.) and telephone numbers
printed in this book are offered as a resource to you. These are not
intended in any way to be or imply an endorsement on the part of the
publishers, nor do we vouch for the content of these sites and numbers
for the life of this book.
Thorndike Press® Large Print Christian Fiction.
The text of this Large Print edition is unabridged.
Other aspects of the book may vary from the original edition.
Set in 16 pt. Plantin.

LIBRARY OF CONGRESS CATALOGING-IN-PUBLICATION DATA

Blackstock, Terri, 1957–
    Downfall / by Terri Blackstock.
        pages ; cm. — (Thorndike Press large print Christian
    fiction) (An intervention novel ; book 3)
        ISBN-13: 978-1-4104-4801-9 (hardcover)
        ISBN-10: 1-4104-4801-0 (hardcover)
        1. Large type books. I. Title.
    PS3552.L34285D69 2012b
    813'.54—dc23   2012006373

Published in 2012 by arrangement with The Zondervan Corporation
LLC.

Printed in Mexico
1 2 3 4 5 6 7 16 15 14 13 12

This book
is lovingly dedicated
to the Nazarene

ACKNOWLEDGMENTS

Since this is the last book in my Intervention Series, I want to thank all of those Christian drug counselors who are called to work with drug addicts and influence their lives for good. We live in a fallen world, full of criminals and drug traffickers, dealers and addicts. But God puts people like you in place to help these confused and devastated people find their way out of the darkness. You invest your lives in them each day, loving them with the love of God, and you help them untangle their messes and learn to live happy, functional lives.

You face many failures, but don't let that discourage you. Your work does have value, even to those who relapse. Your hard work and investment in their lives will bear fruit at some point. It might be soon, but it also might be years from now.

But you're doing the work that God has put on your heart, and your only motivation is that God loves them so much that He was willing to die for them. You're the ones telling them that it's never too late for a second chance. Or a third. Or a hundredth. Like the father in the Prodigal Son story, you are there with your arms open wide, ready to welcome them back into the family.

Please accept my thanks for that. God uses you to give their loved ones hope. You'll never know how broad-reaching and fruitful that hope can be, until you see the result of your labor in heaven.

God bless and encourage you in all of your efforts for Him.

CHAPTER 1

The neighborhood was quiet at 3:00 a.m. Bugs flew in the yellow halo around the street lights, and the half moon gave a gray cast to the coveted homes along the Boulevard. It was the kind of home his mother had dreamed of having, the kind that had always been out of her reach.

The air reeked with greed and ambition. The Avenger, as he liked to call himself, walked in front of those houses, carrying his load in a backpack, thinking maybe he should double back just to blow up some of the BMWs parked in the driveways. Wouldn't it be a thrill to watch from somewhere on the street as businessmen came out of those houses, briefcases in hand, and slipped into their cars? If they all went up at the same time . . . mushroom clouds of fire whooshing over each house in choreographed order . . .

But that was a fantasy for another day.

Today only one car would go up like that.

The Avenger strode around the corner to a street where smaller houses lined the road. Though they weren't as expensive and extravagant as those on the Boulevard, they were still out of his mother's reach. Destined to live in a rotting rat hole, she papered her moldy bathroom with pictures from *Southern Living.* These weren't mansions, but they were big and new. He was sure no mold grew on the attic walls. No cracks ripped the sheetrock in the living rooms. No paint peeled. No sounds of rats scratching through the walls. The people who lived here probably weren't business owners. They were the goons who worked for them, but they were still snotty and superior.

Steam fogged in front of the Avenger's face with every breath as he approached the Covington house. One lamp shone in a room on the side. Out of sight, he'd followed twenty-year-old Emily home a while ago. Now she probably lay tucked in her bed with some feather comforter that cost a mint, smug about her sobriety. Oblivious.

Like always, she hadn't pulled her car into the garage where her mother's car sat. Hers was on the driveway.

The Avenger set his package down beside her car.

10

Right here, under the wheel well . . . that was the best place. He took the jar half-filled with gasoline and the roll of duct tape from his backpack and ripped off enough to tape the bottle under the car, careful not to cover the lamp cord coming from the hole he'd punched in the jar's lid. The gloves on his hands made it difficult work, but he didn't give up. When he'd gotten the bottle in place, he checked to make sure it wasn't leaking. The small amount of gasoline seemed stable. The bottle was angled so it wouldn't leak.

Now if he could just find the right place to connect the other end. He pulled the lamp cord out from under the front of the car, then quietly opened the hood. It made a clicking sound. He froze, looking from left to right. No one stirred at this hour. He shone his flashlight to the place where he needed to connect the cord.

He held the small flashlight in his teeth as he found the spot in the wiring that would ignite his bomb.

The Avenger chuckled to himself as he closed the hood as quietly as possible, pressing down until it engaged. He checked to make sure the cord coming from under the car into the motor wasn't noticeable. If someone knew to look for it, it might be.

But he doubted Emily would see it walking out to her car.

If this worked the way it was supposed to, the bomb would explode when Emily started the car. She would probably escape, but hopefully, she'd be wounded or burned. And she and her family would be terrorized. He'd make them homeless by making them fear their home, and that would just be the beginning.

He chuckled as he gathered his equipment. Then he dropped his gloves into his bag and walked slowly back up the street to where he'd left his car. He reveled in the sense of power his actions had given him. He would never be powerless again.

Too bad he hadn't had an audience tonight. That would have made it so much sweeter. But manipulating victims like chess pieces was almost as good.

It was cold, but the thrill of victory warmed him. He thought about the stash he'd left in his glove compartment, his reward for carrying out his plan. He'd wait until he got home, to the privacy of his basement, and when he was high, he'd go back and carry out the rest of his plan. And what a genius plan it was.

Headlights turned onto the street, illuminating him like a stage star. He pulled up his hood and looked down at the sidewalk as the car slowly passed. As soon as darkness enveloped him again, he broke into a trot back to his car.

There was still so much to do. He had to go take care of Devon, put a gun to her head, watch her bleed. He'd planned it for weeks, waited for the right mixture of courage and cockiness. He'd found it tonight. Freedom had been birthed inside him with one act of will. Now he could set everything right. He'd continue exacting revenge on all those who'd messed with him. So much fallout. So many consequences.

He was the great Avenger.

CHAPTER 2

Emily Covington had managed to slip into the house and down the hall to her bedroom without waking her mother, a major feat since her mom slept lightly when Emily was out. Emily hadn't meant to stay out so late tonight without calling, but one thing had led to another, and she'd wound up coming in at 2:00 a.m., tiptoeing like a high-school kid who'd broken curfew.

Now she had to cram for her test before she could go to bed. Why had she waited until the last minute?

"Emily? You're home?"

She turned to see her mother standing in her bedroom doorway, her hair tangled and disheveled from bed. "Hey. I didn't want to wake you up."

"Did you just come in?"

"A little while ago. Sorry I didn't call. I went to the choir concert at school, and afterward some of us went to a movie. Then we hung out for a while in Ree's dorm room."

"Emily, it's three o'clock, and you have class tomorrow."

"I know. It'll be fine."

"Don't you have a test?"

"Yeah, but it's okay. Just go back to sleep."

Her mother just stood there for a moment. "Okay. Come give me a kiss."

Emily grinned. It was her mother's way of smelling her breath and her hair, to see if she'd been drinking or smoking dope. Emily went to her mom, kissed her cheek, and gave her a hug. "Get a good whiff," she said. "All you'll smell is popcorn and coffee."

Her mother let her go and stared into her eyes, as if checking her pupils for normalcy. "All right, but you're going to put me in an early grave with these long nights."

"Mom, if I lived on campus, you wouldn't even know when I came in."

"Well, you don't live on campus. You live here, and I worry. Go to bed soon, okay?"

"Okay." Emily went back to her bed where her books lay spread out, wishing she hadn't made her mother lose sleep, tonight of all nights. Her mom had a big presentation tomorrow at work, and she wanted her to do well. Her mother had been elated to have this job in Atlanta after they'd struggled so

15

much in Jefferson City. Emily hoped her actions tonight hadn't messed her up.

She resolved to do better next time. The least she could do was call to let her mom know not to worry. But after all she'd put her family through, worry had become a way of life. Staying out so late only exacerbated old memories — and old fears.

But one day Emily would prove to her family that her life of addiction was behind her. Then maybe her mom could sleep better at night.

CHAPTER 3

Milly Prentiss heard the knock on her back door as she waited for her coffeepot to fill. Pulling her robe tighter around her, she stepped to the door and looked through its window onto the rotting back porch. The sun was just coming up, painting the small dirt-patched lawn a lighter shade of gray. She saw no one.

She heard the knock again. Looking lower, she saw the top of a tiny blonde head.

Milly threw the door open. Her next-door neighbor's four-year-old stood in front of her, barefoot and wearing a long gown. There was blood on her sleeves, and the little girl was pale as porcelain.

Milly dropped to her knees. "Allie, honey, what's wrong?"

"Mommy won't wake up."

Milly took the girl's hands. "What's this on your hands?"

The child looked down at her hands

blankly, as if she hadn't noticed it before.

"Allie, what happened?"

"Mommy hurt herself in her bed. I shaked her but she wouldn't come awake."

"Where's Carrie?"

"In her crib, crying. Mommy won't come."

Something thudded in the pit of Milly's stomach. She picked the child up and ran through the yard, her slippers soaking in the cold morning dew. She carried the girl through the carport and into the house, and heard the eighteen-month-old's angry wailing. She put Allie down in front of the couch. "Wait here, honey. I'm going to see about Mommy."

She left Allie in the living room and hurried past the kids' room, to the small bedroom at the end of the short hall. She saw Devon in bed, under the covers, her eyes closed as if she still slept. Milly turned on the light and stepped toward the bed.

The pillow was soaked in blood. Milly gasped and stumbled back. Her neighbor's face was a pale gray, her lips white. Milly forced herself to move closer, touch her arm. Devon's skin was cold.

Milly's mind went blank, and she stood frozen for a moment, unable to move. Carrie's screams penetrated her paralysis.

She had to do something.

She grabbed the phone next to the bed, dialed 911, and choked out the words. "My neighbor is dead in her bed. Please send someone."

CHAPTER 4

The morning was cold and blanketed with fog. Kent Harlan started into his second mile, his breath clouding. He had taken up jogging two years ago when he'd suddenly begun caring how he looked. Before Barbara came into his life, he'd just marked time, letting himself get thick around the middle. Since he'd started running, he'd lost twenty pounds. But he was still nowhere near her league. He wanted to look his best this weekend. The day he got down on one knee would be one of the biggest days of his life.

He hoped Barbara liked the ring.

The fact that she'd moved to Atlanta to be near him nine months ago had changed everything. He felt full of life and hope, with nothing but brightness on the horizon. He wouldn't have believed he could feel young again. He'd tried to take it slow for the sake of Barbara and her kids, allowing them time to get settled here before talking more about marriage. But things seemed to be going pretty well. He couldn't wait much longer.

His cell phone rang, and he slowed and checked the readout. It was the dispatcher at the police department. He and his partner, Andy, were up in the homicide rotation, so he had to take it. He slowed to a walk and clicked on the phone. "Kent Harlan."

"Kent, we've got a homicide at 342 East Bailey Road. Female victim, shot in bed, apparently during a burglary."

"Okay," he said, still breathing hard. "Did you call Andy?"

"I'm calling him next."

"All right. I'll get right over there. Do me a favor and text me that address — I don't have anything to write with."

"Sure thing."

He clicked the phone off and dropped it back into his pocket. He picked up his step again and jogged the rest of the way home. He supposed he should be happy that he'd gotten a whole night's sleep. When he and his partner were next in line to get a case, he was usually disturbed during the night.

He showered, got dressed, and made himself a cup of coffee to take with him. There was no hurry. The first responder was supposed to secure the area, and the body would still be there when he arrived. But he didn't like for much time to pass between the 911 call and his seeing the scene. The more time that passed, and the more investigators who arrived, the more the evidence would be disturbed.

He got his wallet, his pocket change, his car keys. Then he opened the ring box and smiled at the diamond. It was whiter than white, a beautiful flawless stone he'd shopped for weeks for. He took the ring out and put it in his pocket. Just the feel of it made him smile.

It took him twenty minutes to drive across town to the crime scene, in a high-crime residential area where minimum-wage workers lived paycheck to paycheck. He saw the police cars parked in front of the house, and a few neighbors standing in their yards, as if waiting to learn what had happened.

He pulled as close to the house as he could get. Andy must not have gotten here yet; he didn't see his car. Kent got out and trudged across the dewy grass to the side door in the carport, where a uniformed officer stood with a log book.

"What've we got?" Kent asked.

"Woman named Devon Lawrence, thirty years old, shot at point-blank range in her

22

bed. Her four-year-old found her this morning."

The murder suddenly went from routine to tragic in Kent's mind. "A four-year-old? Did the child witness the killing?"

"Doesn't look like it. She says she got up when her baby sister started crying, and went to wake up her mother. She couldn't wake her up, so she went and got the next-door neighbor, Milly Prentiss. Ms. Prentiss is the one who called it in."

"Where are the children now?"

"Next door, still with the neighbor."

"And the father?"

"At work. Miss Prentiss says he works nights at a convenience store. He hasn't been notified yet, but we ought to tell him soon, before one of the neighbors calls him."

Kent stepped into the house and looked around. Tiny kitchen and living room combo, worn, dirty blue carpet, a couch and one chair squeezed in. "Have you figured out the point of entry?"

"Ms. Prentiss said the back door was unlocked, but she thinks that's because the child went out that way. She went in this carport door. She said it was unlocked, too."

Kent saw scratches around the strike plate that suggested someone had picked the lock. He stepped inside, looked around. A purse was lying on the floor, spilled out. No wallet. He scanned the other items in the room. Toys, a diaper bag, a dirty high chair, a flat-screen TV.

"Why would a burglar leave that TV?" he wondered aloud.

"Yeah. Looked odd to me, too."

Kent tried to make that add up. Could be somebody who didn't have a way to carry the TV away. Just wanted fast cash. But why here? What would make him think anyone in this neighborhood had wads of cash lying around?

He looked around for anything else. There was little of value here. The house was in bad shape, with peeling paint and brown leaks on the ceiling. The floor was warped.

He glanced up the hall, saw one of the other officers standing at a bedroom doorway. He headed that way.

In the bed, a young woman lay on her back as if sleeping peacefully, blood soaked into the pillow under her head. There was an entry wound at the center of her forehead. Her eyes were closed. She'd probably been asleep when she was shot. She'd never known what hit her.

At least it had been quick, and the perpetrator hadn't harmed the kids.

He pulled his camera out and snapped

some pictures. The CSIs would take the real crime scene photos, but Kent liked to photograph crime scenes with his own camera, just to make sure nothing had been moved during the investigations.

He heard Andy's voice questioning the cop at the carport door. Kent glanced at the cop near him, still standing back, looking a little shaken. "What do we know about the husband?"

"The neighbor says he has drug problems. Has been in rehab. They have a history of domestic violence, but the police have never been called about it. He's on probation for a drug charge."

So the husband had the history and the mental capacity to do this.

Andy came to the doorway and looked inside. "Morning, guys."

Kent nodded at him, then turned back to the cop. "Did the neighbor hear the gunshot?"

"No. She says she didn't hear anything until the kid knocked on her door."

He pictured a four-year-old child running through the yard to get help for her mother. His stomach twisted. Surely a father wouldn't murder the mother and let his child find her. But if he was strung out, who knew what he was capable of?

"Andy, let's go talk to the neighbor. Then we'll see what the husband has to say. He's at work, supposedly. Hasn't been notified."

"You think he already knows?"

"Could be." He clicked his phone on as he walked out of the house, dialed the department, and asked a police sergeant to run a rap sheet on the husband — William Lawrence, who went as Bo — and email it to him. He would try to open the file with his iPhone.

They crossed the yard and knocked on the door to the ramshackle house next door. A little woman of about sixty answered.

"Miss Prentiss?"

"Yes," she said.

Her eyes were red-rimmed and puffy, her nose crimson. She'd clearly had a bad morning. "I'm Detective Kent Harlan, Atlanta Homicide. This is my partner, Andy Joiner. Could we come in and talk to you?"

"Yes, but please — don't upset the children," she said in a low voice. "I've fed them and calmed them down."

Kent stepped into the house. The little girl sat at the table, coloring on a piece of yellow legal paper. The baby sat on the floor, playing with plastic blocks.

Milly went to pick the baby up. "Poor little thing was crying and crying," she said softly.

The little girl was still wearing her gown with bloody sleeves, and her feet were bare. "I need to talk to the child," he whispered to Milly.

She looked distressed, but nodded.

He went to the table, pulled out a chair. "Hi," he said.

The little girl looked up at him with soulful eyes as he sat down. Mucus had crusted under her nose. "Hi," she said.

"I'm Kent. What's your name?"

"Allie."

"Allie, can you tell me what happened when you woke up this morning?"

Her bottom lip puckered out, and tears filled her eyes. "Mommy died."

"Did you hear any noise?"

"No."

"Did you hear her talking to anybody? Did you see anybody in the house?"

"No. She wouldn't talk because she wouldn't wake up."

"So you didn't hear a loud bang?"

She frowned, thinking. "I dreamed about a loud bang sound."

"Dreamed it?" Kent asked. "Did it wake you up?"

"I don't know."

This wasn't easy. The child probably heard the gunshot in her sleep, but didn't wake all the way.

"What made you get up?"

"Carrie crying."

"Nothing else?"

She shook her head and went back to coloring.

Kent tried one more time. "Allie, did you hear Carrie crying right after the bang?"

"No," she said. "The bang was a dream, but the crying was real. It was later."

He'd know more when the medical examiner figured out the time of death. He looked up at Ms. Prentiss. "Ma'am, did you hear a gunshot?"

"No, but I have sleep apnea. I sleep with a CPAP, and it makes noise. I sleep pretty deep. I hadn't been up very long when Allie came."

"What can you tell us about Mr. Lawrence?" Andy asked.

"I don't like him very much," she said in a low voice. "He's had a problem with cocaine. Got arrested a few months ago, spent a little time in jail. Then they let him go to rehab. He's only been out a few months."

"Has he been using again?"

"Not that I know of. Devon told me he was doing good. That he was sober and going to work every night. She said he hadn't been mean lately."

The other officer had mentioned domestic violence. He'd probably gotten that information from her. "Mean, how?"

"I would hear them yelling sometimes. Couple of times I saw bruises. He broke her nose once, but even then she never would call the police. She finally did call them when she found a big stash of dope in her house and the baby almost got into it. Made her mad enough to turn him in. That's when he was arrested."

Kent met Andy's eyes. If the wife was responsible for her husband's jail time and probation, he might have gotten even tonight. "Where does he work?"

"At that convenience store at the Exxon station. It's called J.R.'s 24/7."

Kent hoped they'd learn more from visiting the husband and gauging his reaction to his wife's death.

"Do you think this person might come back?" she asked. "I live alone, and I'm nervous."

"We don't know, ma'am. But we're going to do our best to find him."

"But how did the person get in? Do you think it was Bo?" she whispered, glancing at Allie as if making sure she couldn't hear.

Kent didn't answer. "We're looking at all

the evidence, but we don't have answers just yet."

"What am I supposed to do with the kids? I need to clean Allie up, but I can't get in there to get her clothes."

"We'll get something for her to wear, and have someone come and take care of them until we can get a family member to pick them up."

"No, that's okay. They know me. I baby-sit them a lot. I'll keep them until their daddy or grandma comes." She burst into tears and covered her face. "This is so awful. Poor Devon!"

He resisted the urge to comfort her, but he hoped someone would. When he and Andy stepped outside, he heard the teary-eyed woman lock her deadbolt.

"I'm betting on the husband," Andy said. "What do you bet he can't prove he was at work all night?"

"We'll soon find out."

Kent left Andy working the crime scene. Driving to the convenience store, he considered the possibility that the husband wasn't involved. He felt the burning in his gut that he always felt when he had to break the news of a murder to a family member. It was the part of the job he hated most.

He found the place, an old, peeling structure with burglar bars on the windows. The store was lit up, and beyond the glass was a man behind the counter, sitting on a stool and watching the television over his head.

He got out of his car and pushed through the glass doors.

"You doin' all right?" the man asked as Kent approached. He looked sober. His eyes were clear, though he looked tired.

"Are you Bo Lawrence?" Kent asked.

The man crossed his arms. Defensive. Guarded. "Yeah, why?"

"I'm with the Atlanta Police Department, Homicide Division."

The man's face changed, and deep lines in his skin caught the shadows cast by the dusty light. "Homicide? What happened?"

"We had a call to your house this morning. Your wife had been shot."

Kent watched Bo's face. Bo swallowed, his Adam's apple bobbing. It was hard to say whether his face changed color — he was already pale. "Shot? She's okay, though, right?"

"I'm afraid not. She didn't make it."

Bo's mouth fell open, and he couldn't speak for a moment. He brought both hands to his greasy hair, slid his dirty fingers through. "But . . . we don't have guns in the house. We don't . . . who . . . what happened?"

"It appears to be a burglary. Someone came in and shot her in her sleep."

He almost choked with his intake of breath. "The girls . . . my children . . . are they . . . ?"

"They're fine. Your daughter Allie found your wife."

He wavered as though he might faint, and reached out to grab the counter. "Allie? Who did this?" he whispered loudly.

Kent kept his voice steady. "We wanted to notify you and find out who we could call about your children."

"Where are they now?" he asked, his face twisting in what looked like genuine anguish.

"They're with Milly Prentiss, next door."

He nodded. "Milly . . . that's good."

There were no tears, but that wasn't unusual. Getting news of a murder was shocking, and people responded in different ways. "Who . . . who called the police?"

The question was odd. It wasn't the first thing most people thought to ask. "Milly did, after your daughter went to her."

"So . . . did she see who did it?"

"No, I'm afraid not. I'd like for you to come to the station, so we could talk to you about this. Maybe you could give us some leads."

He looked down at the cash register. "Yeah . . . of course. I have to call my boss. I'll have to close the store."

Kent looked around. "How long have you been on shift tonight?"

At first, the man didn't seem to hear. He stared into space, as if sorting through the news. "Uh . . . since 8:00 last night. I'm working a twelve-hour shift."

"Have you left at all?"

The man picked up the phone, but he didn't dial. "No, not at all. I've been here all night. Haven't even gone out to smoke. I've been trying to quit."

Kent's eyes went to the security cameras on the ceiling behind the counter. He could get the video and confirm that what the man said was true.

"Look, I know the first person you always think of is the husband." His voice sounded shredded, raspy. "But I swear . . . I loved my wife. I wouldn't do anything to hurt her." He brought his hand to his mouth, trembling, as his grief etched deeper into his face. Nothing unusual in his reaction.

After talking to his boss, Bo locked down the store and turned off all the lights. Kent retrieved the security video with no objection from him. Then Bo followed Kent out to the car and got into the front passenger seat. There were still no tears as Kent drove him to the station. When they got there, Kent watched the video footage. It confirmed Bo's story. He had been at work all night.

The guy was probably just a grieving husband in shock, but Kent hoped he had some information that would lead them to his wife's killer.

CHAPTER 5

"Emily, you've got to stop staying up so late when you have school the next morning." Barbara slid the cereal box across the counter at her bleary-eyed daughter.

"I can't help it," Emily said in a hoarse, groggy voice. "I can't get to sleep any earlier."

"It's her nature, Mom," Lance said, chomping on his Cheerios. "She's a party girl to the bone."

"Shut up," Emily muttered. "I wasn't partying."

Barbara dug into her purse for lunch money for Lance and laid it on the counter. "I'm just saying, Emily, that you have to fight addictive behaviors like staying up all night when you have school. You have to learn to think ahead, not just do what feels right in the moment."

"It's not an addictive behavior, Mom. Everybody I know stays up late. It's a college thing."

"And that's why half the student body drops out before they get a degree." Barbara glanced at Lance, her sixteen-year-old. "Lance, promise me you'll eat lunch today."

He didn't answer, just pretended to be engrossed in the writing on the cereal box.

"Lance, did you hear me?"

"Yes. But I hate lunch."

"You hate *lunch*?" Emily asked. "That's stupid. You hate gym or math or science. Nobody hates lunch."

"They do if they have to sit by themselves."

"I thought your girlfriend sat with you," Emily said.

"April's not my girlfriend. At least, not yet." He brought his milk to his mouth, eyes grinning as he drank. He set the glass down too hard. "She doesn't always sit with me. Sometimes she skips lunch. Why can't I just be homeschooled?"

They'd been all through this. "Lance, you'll make friends," Barbara said. "Just hang in there."

"I had plenty of friends in Jeff City."

They'd moved here in January, after selling their house in Missouri. Lance had been recovering from a serious injury to his lung at the time, and he'd had a hard time fitting in after changing schools midyear. Since he hadn't bonded with anyone by the time school was out for the summer, he'd had a long, lonely three months. Baseball used to be his pastime during those hot months, and it was a way to make friends, but since his lung capacity wasn't back to a hundred percent and he didn't know anyone well, he hadn't signed up. Barbara regretted not talking him into it. "You were a popular guy back home, and you will be again. And you'll be stronger for it. You're learning new skills. Compassion for lonely people, for one. Good things can come of this. Moving here was right for the family."

"No, it was right for *you,* so you could be closer to Kent. I get that, and I like him and all. But I miss my friends. I never hated going to school before this. Those jocks treat me like the biggest dork in Georgia. I thought this fall might be better, but nothing has changed since school started back."

Emily seemed to be coming awake now as she nursed her coffee. "They're just jealous. Some cute new guy comes in and invades their territory, and the girls take notice."

"April's the only girl taking notice, and she treats me like a brother. Trust me, *they* all think I'm a dork, too. I came to school skinny and sick, and that's how they'll keep seeing me."

"You're not a dork." Barbara leaned across the counter, touched Lance's chin. "Look at me, son."

He met her eyes.

"You're a hero. A life-saver. You know who you are. Don't let them convince you that you're anything else."

"Yeah, well, they think I made it all up."

"It doesn't matter what they think," Emily said. "We know what happened."

Barbara looked down at her son's chest. His breathing was still more labored than it used to be. She worried about him. Sometimes she considered moving back to Missouri just to make his life easier.

But she could barely make a living in Jefferson City, and Emily had way too many drug triggers there. And yes, she liked living near Kent. They'd grown closer since she'd moved here, and it looked like they might have a future together.

She'd been adrift since her husband died six years ago. Kent had brought joy to her life and a new outlook. He'd also helped her land a job here working as an interior designer for an architectural firm. It was a dream come true — and she was good at it. She was making even more money than she'd made during the best years of having her own business. She had so much debt from Emily's drug days and the decline in her business, that the extra income was much needed. Her head was above water for the first time in years.

"Can you at least give me a ride to school this morning?" Lance asked Emily. "I hate riding the stupid bus."

"Can't," Emily said. "I'm running late. I have to leave in a few minutes and I won't have time to take you. Test today."

"If I had a car my life wouldn't be so miserable."

Barbara smiled. "It won't be that much longer." He'd worked all summer mowing lawns to earn as much as he could, and she had agreed to match whatever he raised. But that still wouldn't be enough to pay for a reliable vehicle.

Thankfully, Lance didn't ask Barbara to take him to school. She had to go in early, too — to get her ducks in a row before her big presentation today. They were bidding on a new sanctuary for Three Roads Baptist Church, one of the largest Baptist churches in Atlanta. The architects depended on her to sell the deacon leadership and church's senior staff on her colors, finishes, stained glass, and ideas for the architectural details that would make it a glorious place to worship.

In spite of her fatigue from last night, she was ready. If nothing went wrong, they would surely get this account.

CHAPTER 6

Emily felt guilty walking out to her car. Lance stood at the end of the driveway, waiting for the big yellow torture chamber they called a bus.

She got in and put her coffee cup in the drink holder, her books on the seat. She adjusted her rearview mirror, turned the ignition —

A *pop* shook the car, startling her. Suddenly, she saw Lance waving at her, arms arching wildly over his head. Confused, she rolled her passenger window down. "What is it?"

"Fire!" Lance yelled. "Get out!"

Emily jumped out. Smoke, white and thick, floated out from under her car, and as she stumbled back, she saw the small flames, way too close to the gas tank. Lance dropped his backpack and dashed into the garage, then reappeared with a fire extinguisher.

Emily stood back as he sprayed foam at the origin of the fire under the car. It went out, leaving only a cloud of smoke.

Out of breath, Lance leaned into the car and turned off the engine. His cheeks were mottled red as he stumbled back. Emily gaped at the car, stunned. "What *was* that?"

She hit the concrete and looked under her car. There was duct tape stuck to the wheel well, broken glass scattered in the foam, the smell of gas. A cord ran from the duct tape to the front of the car. Lance bent down and crawled closer. "Dude, that's a bomb!"

No way. Something must have come loose . . . a wire . . . a belt . . . But duct tape? Emily moved into the foam and reached for the cord, but Lance grabbed her hand. "Don't touch it. Call the police. They should see it just like that. Want me to call Kent?"

"No, I'll call 911." But she didn't. Instead, she just crouched there, staring. A bomb under her car? Who would do that? It could have killed her if the flames had gotten to the fuel tank. Why would someone want her car to explode?

She heard the rumble of the school bus a couple of blocks up the street. "Bus is coming," Lance said. "But I'm not going. I'm staying with you."

42

Emily didn't argue. She didn't want to be here alone if someone was trying to kill her. What if there was another booby trap somewhere?

She got her purse out of the car and dug out her phone. Would the police even believe her, if they knew of her past? Her face had been all over the news here when she was missing two years ago, and lots of people still remembered her. Her DUIs in Jeff City would be on their computers like neon reminders that she used to live dangerously.

Swallowing the fear, she made the call to 911. When she was assured that the police were on their way, she handed her phone to Lance. "Will you call Mom and tell her?"

Lance took the phone as the bus squeaked to a stop. He waved it by. The voices of the kids faded as the bus huffed past.

Emily's mind raced as he called their mother. This couldn't be real. Someone was playing a joke on her. It couldn't be a real bomb, just a smoke bomb, something to scare her. There was no one in Atlanta who would deliberately want to hurt her, was there?

Back in Jefferson City, she'd run with a pretty rough crowd. She'd even made a few drug dealers mad when she went into their lair and dragged a friend out last year. But

Jeff City was five hundred miles away, and almost a year had passed since then.

She heard Lance connecting with her mother. "Mom? You're not gonna believe what happened. I'm standing here waiting for the bus and Emily gets in her car, and . . ."

Arms crossed, she paced up the driveway, avoiding the foam on the concrete, and tried to think. Yes, she had a few friends in the drug culture here, but only because she worked part-time at a local rehab. She'd needed a job when she moved here, but people were reluctant to hire her. Though she'd been cleared of any wrongdoing after her face was plastered all over the news, people weren't entirely sure that she was trustworthy. Some of them couldn't remember how the case had ended. They only knew that she'd been a suspect in a woman's death.

Then she'd had the idea to apply at the Haven House Treatment Center not far from her area of town, and they'd hired her to work in the office on Saturdays. Some of the clients could be unpredictable if they were using again after graduating from the program. Some might even resent her being part of the staff that controlled their lives for twelve weeks. But she was never in charge. She only checked visitors in and out, answered the phones, and searched and breathalyzed clients when they came back from passes.

Would anyone come after her now to *kill* her? She shivered, though the air was muggy and warm. Where were the police?

"Emily, Mom wants to talk to you."

Sighing, she took the phone. "Hey."

"Emily, what's going on?" Panic, anger, and accusation rippled in her voice.

Emily bit back the urge to defend herself. "I don't know. The police are on their way. The fire department, too."

There was a pregnant silence, then her mother blurted it out. "Emily, what have you dragged us into now?"

The words hit her harder than the bomb had. She heard sirens in the distance. "Mom, I don't know what's going on! I didn't drag us into anything!"

"People don't put bombs under your car for no reason! Have you been hanging out with those people again?"

"*What* people?"

"Drug dealers! Crazy addicts!"

"Mom, you know I haven't."

"I knew when you were staying out so late that something wasn't right. And working in that place with all that temptation."

45

Emily couldn't take anymore. She saw the fire trucks turning onto her street. "Mom, I've gotta go. They're here."

She clicked off the phone, knowing it would only set her mother off, and walked to the end of the driveway to meet them.

CHAPTER 7

Barbara ran two red lights and a stop sign getting back to her house. As she rounded the corner to her block, she saw the police cars and fire trucks parked against her curb. Her throat constricted, and acid burned her stomach.

She stopped behind one of the police cars, saw the foam on the ground and the charred places lapping up from the undercarriage of Emily's car. Emily could have been killed!

She burst out of the car as Lance came toward her. "Mom, it was strapped on with duct tape. Had a cord going to the engine."

The idea of someone stalking into their driveway and tampering with Emily's car made Barbara speechless. She went to Emily, pulled her into a rough hug, then stepped back and looked at her eyes. Was this a sign of relapse? Crazy, inexplicable things happened all the time when Emily was using. They didn't happen to people who led sober, orderly lives. "Are you okay?"

"Yeah. If Lance hadn't been here, I don't know what would have happened."

Barbara turned back to the car. "Emily, *who did this?*"

Emily looked self-consciously at the cop she'd been talking to. "Mom, if I knew I would tell them."

Barbara stepped toward the crime scene investigator who lay on his back on a tarp, taking pictures of the bomb residue under the car. "What kind of bomb was it?"

"Homemade device," he said. "Pretty crude. A cord and a jar of gas, rigged to spark when the ignition was turned. Could have been a lot worse."

The uniformed cop standing near the car turned to Emily. "Has anybody threatened you lately? Anybody who might have something against you?"

She swept her hair behind her ear. "No, I can't think of anybody."

"Anyone you might owe money to?"

"No, no one at all."

"Do you gamble? Use drugs?"

"No, neither." Emily gave her mom a guilty glance. "I did have a drug problem," she added, "but I've been sober for about two years. I can promise you that I haven't used since we moved here, so I don't have any drug connections here."

"Other than the ones at the rehab," Barbara said.

The officer's expression turned critical. "You're still in rehab?"

Emily huffed and shot her mother an angry look. "I'm not *in* the rehab she's talking about. I *work* at Haven House."

"I knew she shouldn't take that job," Barbara said. "I knew this was bad news, being around other addicts who —"

"Mom, stop!" Emily's cheeks blotched crimson. "Stop freaking out!" She turned back to the cop. "I don't really counsel the clients or anything. I work in the office on Saturdays. Answer the phone, check out visitors, give breathalyzer checks when people have passes. Nothing that would make anybody want to kill me." She checked her watch. "I have a test in a few minutes. Am I gonna be able to drive my car?"

"No!" Barbara cried. "Emily, it was on fire! You can't just hop in it and take off."

"Then what am I gonna do? Dr. Ingles won't let me make it up without a doctor's excuse."

"We'll get a police excuse. It'll have to do. They'll tell him you couldn't take the test because someone tried to blow you up!"

Emily grunted. "I can't tell him *that*."

"So you're in college?" the cop asked her. "Is there anyone at school you've made mad? Any rivals?"

"No!" she said. "Really, I can't think of a single person."

Barbara wasn't satisfied. "You have to find who did this. We won't be able to sleep at night. Someone came into our driveway . . . they wanted to kill her." She thought of the danger Emily had been in two years ago, when a maniac had come so close to ending her life. But he was dead. It couldn't have been him.

How could this be happening again? She'd believed the danger was behind them. She studied her daughter's eyes again. Emily had been coming in so late at night. Staying up into the wee hours. She hung out with college kids who were testing their wings, probably hanging out in clubs, and others in recovery whom she'd met in AA. She claimed the group kept her anchored and gave her the necessary support to stay sober. Barbara had seen the positive results, so she'd put aside her fears and allowed her to do whatever would help her stay clean. But what if one of them had lured Emily back into drugs?

Her life was so fragile.

Drug dealers did things like this. Drive-by

shootings. Revenge executions. Car bombs weren't common or she would have heard about them more on the news, but if someone was trying to get her to pay money she owed and wanted to scare her . . .

"Maybe it was just some kid pulling a prank," Lance said, cutting into her thoughts.

Yes, a kid! She dragged her renegade thoughts back. Just some neighborhood punk who'd picked their house at random. Barbara brought a hand to her forehead. "Are we even safe in this house? Is this person going to come back?"

"We're examining the evidence. He probably left fingerprints. Hopefully we'll be able to track him down soon."

"But fingerprints would only help if it was someone who had a record, right? What if this person isn't in the system?"

"Trace evidence can still help us identify the perpetrator. We'll do our best to find him."

She paced up the driveway, massaging her temples.

"Mom," Lance said, "get a grip. Let them do their job. Why don't you go in and sit down until they're finished?"

"It's a bomb!" she shouted, her voice cracking. "Someone tried to kill your sister.

Don't *tell* me to get a grip!"

Why was she yelling at her son? Lance was just trying to calm her down. But she couldn't be calm.

Barbara decided to call Kent. He should be told about this. At the very least, he could make sure the police followed up. Maybe he could even solve it himself.

CHAPTER 8

The rat-tat-tat of the Avenger's fingers did a drumbeat with the rap song blaring from his radio as he drove to the street where the Covingtons lived. If he was lucky, he'd see police cars and fire trucks there with ambulances, just like he'd seen at the murder scene. He loved the power. He, alone, had caused all this commotion, and had police teams dispatched to two separate areas on the same morning.

And they didn't yet know the half of it. As he drove, he imagined the pain Emily was suffering. Possible burns on her lovely, fair skin. The disfigurement of that pretty face of hers. The fear that he would be back . . .

He felt a thrill as he turned onto her street and saw two police cars and a fire truck lined up out front. He laughed and turned the music down so he wouldn't call attention to himself. Shoving on sunglasses so he wouldn't be recognized, he drove by at a normal speed.

Emily stood in the front yard with foam on the ground near her like newly fallen snow. She wasn't harmed at all. Clearly, they'd put the fire out before anyone got hurt.

Okay. That was fine. The bomb had worked, anyway.

He tried to think what would happen now. They wouldn't be able to trace the bomb back to him. He'd been careful to avoid leaving fingerprints. It was just a bottle, gasoline, duct tape, and an electrical cord. Nothing that could identify him.

Emily would be paranoid now, constantly looking over her shoulder, fearing whoever was trying to kill her. And that was what he wanted. She and her sweet little family would be living in fear.

He'd enjoy playing with them for a while before he finally ended it.

Laughing aloud, he ramped his music back up, drove a few miles away, then pulled into an alley and snorted a line. He was superhuman, in control, sovereign over his subjects. Invincible and unstoppable. He hadn't slept in two days — not since he'd declared his freedom — and didn't remember when he'd last eaten. He didn't require

what ordinary mortals needed to survive.
Life had never been more fun.

CHAPTER 9

Kent had ignored the phone vibrating in his pocket as he interviewed Bo Lawrence about his wife's background. Whoever it was could wait until he was finished.

But then Rick, the front desk sergeant, stuck his head into the interview room. "Kent, Barbara's on the phone. She says it's an emergency."

That never happened. Barbara understood that if she called and he didn't answer, he was in a situation in which he couldn't take the call. For her to call the police precinct and tell Rick it was an emergency . . . something had to be seriously wrong.

He excused himself, stepped out of the room, and asked Rick to get Bo a bottle of water or coffee. The man had shed quite a few tears since reality had sunk in, and was probably getting dehydrated and thirsty. If they kept him comfortable, he'd be more willing to talk.

He found a quiet place in the stairwell, pulled out his cell phone, and sat on the steps as he dialed Barbara's number.

She answered quickly. "Kent?"

"Hey, babe. Sorry I haven't been answering. I was working a case —"

She didn't wait for him to finish. "Someone planted a homemade bomb under Emily's car —"

He sprang to his feet. *"What?"*

She spilled out the story, her voice raspy with tears. He couldn't stand the thought of her so distraught. "Kent, I don't know what's going on. She's been staying out late and hanging out with AA friends —"

"That doesn't mean she's relapsed, Barbara. She's a college kid. They stay out late."

"But this is crazy. It's one of those drug-addict things, you know? Ridiculous, inexplicable things happening to her. I don't know what to do."

Kent glanced back toward the interview room. He supposed he could let the husband go and pick up with him again later. The man should probably look in on his kids, talk to his wife's family . . .

"Look, I'm coming over. Tell the men who are there to wait for me. I want to see the scene, talk to the CSI."

"Good. We have to find who did this

before they really hurt her."

"We will." He pushed through the door back into the precinct room. "So she wasn't burned or hurt in any way?"

"No. She's just shaken up."

"That's a miracle," he said. "God's looking out for the kid. Just remember that. I'll be there in a few minutes."

He cut off the phone, went back to the interview room. Bo had already finished off his water, and sat with his face in his hands. "Bo, I'm gonna let you go now, but stay around the area in case I need to talk to you again. And if you think of anything else we should know, or if you hear anything that could be a lead on this case, call me at this number." He handed Bo a card with his cell phone number on it.

Bo got up, moving slowly, as if walking through water. As if he didn't know where to go, who to talk to, what to do.

"You should probably notify your wife's family," Kent said.

Bo nodded. "Yeah, I will." The man just stood there, staring into space.

"You okay?"

"Yeah, I . . . just don't have my car here, so . . ."

"I'll get one of our men to take you back to your car at the store. You can't go into the house yet, though. They're still working the scene."

He rubbed his face, his mouth trembling. "Can I see her?"

They hadn't yet moved the body from where she'd been found. "No, not yet, but we'll have someone call you as soon you can."

Bo nodded, staring vacantly, as if searching his mind for a starting point to tackling this nightmare. Kent made arrangements to get him to wherever he wanted to go, then hurried out to his own car and headed for Barbara's house.

CHAPTER 10

The test had been over for an hour by the time Emily got to school. She parked farther away than she was used to, since the parking lot filled up early, then tromped across campus to the administration building, where her history professor kept an office. He had a stern policy — no missed tests without a doctor's excuse — but she clutched her police report in her hand, hoping he would make an exception just this once. Could he give as much weight to a murder attempt as he did to the flu?

She found Dr. Ingles in his office, his door open as he sat hunched over test papers. He was a large man with a bald head and hefty paunch, and he wore a perpetual scowl. She had never had a conversation with him outside of class, so her mouth went dry. She cleared her throat and knocked on the door's casing.

He looked up at her, then leaned back

hard. "Well, well, Miss Covington. Glad to see you finally made it to school today."

She drew in a deep breath and reminded herself that Georgians liked to hear ma'am and sir. If she could just remember to say it. "Sir, may I talk to you?"

"You missed your test, Miss Covington. That's unfortunate."

She couldn't tell him straight out that someone had tried to kill her. She didn't want this igniting the gossip mill like wildfire. "I was leaving on time this morning, when my car caught fire. My brother waved me down and I got out before I was hurt, but I had to wait for the fire department and the police —"

His bushy eyebrows shot up. "The police?"

"Yes . . . sir." Why couldn't she just say it naturally? But the awkward *sir* didn't seem to bother him. He suddenly looked interested.

"They came with the fire department. I have the police report here. It's not a doctor's excuse, but it proves that it happened."

He took the report, and she hoped he would just look at the date and time and not read the officer's scribbled handwriting at the bottom. But that was exactly where his gaze swept. She held her breath as he picked up his glasses and shoved them on, frowning as he read.

"They were there forever," she said in a soft voice, as if calming a rabid animal. "I told them I had a test, but I had to stay until they were finished, and then the car had to be towed and I had to work out another ride. I couldn't drive it like that."

He didn't seem to be listening. "Wait a moment," he said, looking up from the yellow copy of the report. "Sit down. Start over."

At least he was going to hear her out. She went in and sat down, set her books on the seat next to her. His office wasn't what she often saw in college professors' offices. His was relatively neat, free of dust, and a shiny green plant of some kind sat under his window, cared for. He had a child's pictures tacked on a bulletin board and taped to the back of his door. His grandchild's drawings? He seemed too old to have small children of his own. Maybe he wasn't as scary as he seemed.

"Sounds like you've had a hair-raising morning. Just take a breath and start over."

Only then did she realize she was still shaking. "Dr. Ingles, I've really tried to do well in this class. I study and read everything we're asked to read, and I like history. It's interesting, like a novel. I was ready for this test. But I didn't expect the fire —"

"It sounds as if it was more than a fire. It says something about a bomb?"

She swallowed and looked down at her hands. "Okay, but I'd rather this didn't get around. I have . . . a reputation already. But somebody taped a bomb to the bottom of my car, and when I started it, it caught fire."

He asked her a few questions, and she answered them as briefly as she could. "But I hope you can see that this was out of my control. Will you please let me make up the test?"

He took off his glasses and handed the police report back to her. "Miss Covington . . ."

She wanted to tell him to call her Emily, but professors had a thing about using your last name. It made her uncomfortable, like he was talking to her mother instead of her.

"I know about your history. I followed the news stories when you were missing. I recognized you the first day you were in my class."

She looked at her feet. "Great."

He leaned forward and studied her until she met his eyes. "I've been inspired by your turnaround. You seem very diligent and focused now, and I find that refreshing. But this is disturbing."

"Tell me about it," she said. "My mom is all freaking out because she thinks if somebody's trying to kill me I must have gone back to drugs. But I haven't. I'm at this school every day, and I'm keeping a B average. Trust me — when I was using, I didn't make As and Bs. I didn't even show up for school. A lot of the time I didn't even qualify for Fs. I'm working really hard to stay sober, and I don't think about drugs all the time anymore. This isn't my fault. But meanwhile, I've missed an important test. Please, will you let me take a make-up?"

"So you feel you were ready for it this morning?"

"Yes. Absolutely. I can take it right now."

He stared at her, his gaze so piercing that she almost felt he could read her thoughts. "All right, Miss Covington. I have another class taking the test at noon in the same room. You can take it with them."

She let out her breath. "Thank you so much." She got her books, stood. "I really appreciate it."

"Be careful."

"I will," she said. "I'll see you at noon."

She punched the air with a victorious fist as she left his office. Then she pulled out her phone and texted her mother. *He's let-*

ting me make up the test at noon!

Her second class today wasn't until one, so she had time to go to the library and focus her thoughts. If she could quit thinking about the bomb, maybe she could even pass the test.

CHAPTER 11

Barbara had loaned her car to Emily, so Kent drove her to work. He wished he could calm her fears. She had missed an important pre-presentation meeting this morning, and that wouldn't make her look good at work. And complicating her situation further, Kent had strongly suggested that each of them keep quiet about the bomb, explaining only on a need-to-know basis. Whoever had done this was clearly looking for some kind of power, and he probably wanted word to get around. Better to have as little press and word of mouth as possible.

Kent suspected that the bomber hadn't really wanted to kill Emily. If he had, it would have been easy enough to do it. According to the CSI who'd worked the scene, the bomb must not have held much gasoline. If it had, the fuel tank would have gone up.

No, whoever did this had been trying to

jerk her around.

"Are you gonna be okay?" he asked Barbara as they approached her office building.

"Yeah, I have to be. This is a huge presentation. I can't drop the ball on it."

"But you're ready, right?"

"I think so. The presentation is at noon. The deacon leadership and church staff are coming to our offices for a catered lunch, and we're presenting it then." She looked out the window, and he knew where her mind was going. "Kent, what if she's using again? I really don't think I can go through that again."

"Emily looks fine. But I never saw her when she was high."

"But this staying out until all hours . . . I haven't wanted to give her a curfew because she's twenty, and I know that if she were in the dorm, she'd stay out late anyway. I wanted her to stay home for just this reason. I want to make sure she's solid enough in her sobriety before she lives away from home."

"Other than the late hours, you've had no reason to suspect her. You check her when she comes in, don't you?"

"Yeah, but . . . how do you tell the difference between sleepy and loaded?"

"You can tell, Barbara. You've told me

yourself that when she was using, she didn't bathe, didn't change clothes, didn't brush her teeth or her hair. She was a mess, didn't go to school, didn't come home. She's not like that now."

"No, she's not." She took his hand, stroked it with her thumb. "You're helping. I appreciate your perspective."

"Well, if you're still suspicious, drug-test her tonight."

She sighed. "I don't know how she'd take that."

"Her reaction will be telling. If she balks, then you'll know she could be using. If she's really sober, she'll want to prove it. I can bring you a test kit tonight if you want."

Barbara nodded. "I guess so." She sighed. "I hope the insurance company will pay for a rental until we can get her car checked out. I don't like having to depend on you."

Kent smiled. "I like it when I can help."

"But you were working a case, weren't you?"

"Yeah. A woman found dead in her bed this morning. She had two little kids. I had to tell her husband."

Barbara gaped at him. "Kent, I'm so sorry to pull you away from that."

"No problem. I can get back to it now."

"I'll get Emily to pick me up this afternoon if we haven't gotten a rental by then."

He turned into the parking lot and drove her to the front door. "Call me if you can't."

"I'll call a cab before I'll take you away from hunting down a killer."

"I can take a minute to pick you up, Barbara."

She hesitated before getting out. "Do you think they got enough evidence to figure out who planted the bomb?"

"I hope so. I'll stay on top of that too, babe. I'll keep you informed. Let me know immediately if anything else happens."

She kissed him lightly, and he watched her get out and waited until she was inside. Though he had been interrupted on his murder case, there was something he liked about being needed by a group of people he loved. They weren't his family yet, but he felt like they were.

He shifted in his seat and slid his hand into his pocket, felt for the ring. It was still there. When should he ask her? The middle of a puzzling murder case wasn't the right time. And the bomb added another element of distraction. No, he wanted to ask her in a way that was memorable, when there was nothing that would shipwreck her joy.

Driving back to the murder scene, he said a silent prayer that Emily's circumstances this morning didn't herald a relapse. If she had stumbled and was using again, the repercussions would be much further reaching than she knew.

Barbara didn't deserve that. She'd already been through way more than any mother should endure.

CHAPTER 12

Lance hated going into history late, especially when it was full of football players who loved making him look stupid.

The door was closed, so he knocked, then stepped inside. Mr. Herman turned mid-sentence and held out his hand for Lance's admittance slip. Lance gave it to him. "Sorry I'm late," he muttered.

"Care to explain why you are?" Mr. Herman asked.

Lance wanted to say no, that he'd prefer not to talk in front of the whole stinking class, but that would only drag it out. He decided just to blurt it. "My sister's car caught fire. Big family drama. Fire trucks and everything."

There. It wasn't the whole story, but enough to get him off the hook.

"That sounds like a valid excuse," Herman said.

There was a snicker across the class.

"Lance has lots of family drama," Randall, the second-string quarterback, said. "He's a big superhero, you know."

Lance felt the heat in his cheeks as he dropped into his seat.

"Yeah, Mr. Herman, he's a CIA agent and spends his spare time fighting crime and rescuing damsels in distress."

The class laughed. Lance ground his molars but didn't speak. April Pullen, his friend who sat behind him, patted his shoulder.

"He was shot in the heart just a few months ago," the tight end said.

"With a silver bullet," Randall spouted.

Lance had learned months ago not to respond when they started down this road. But April spoke up. "Not the heart, the lungs."

"Oh, yeah," the quarterback said. "The lungs. He was dead for four days, and then miraculously revived, so he could return to his life of saving the world from crime."

"And then these Martians landed in his backyard and beamed him up."

The class was enjoying this. Lance grinned, pretending he enjoyed it, too. "Randall knows 'cause he was beamed up with me. Too bad about those brain experiments they did on him."

Now the class laughed with him.

"All right, that's enough, guys," Herman said. "Lance, we're glad you made it. I was just telling the students that we're fixing to have a little quiz tomorrow."

Great. Lance got his book out of his backpack and opened it. He didn't even know what chapter they were in. How would he ever pass a quiz?

After class, he took his time packing his binder and book back in his backpack, hoping his tormenters would clear out before he left the room.

"You okay?" April asked him.

Lance shrugged. "Sure. Just a bad morning."

"Don't let them get to you. They're jerks."

More than once, he'd thought of showing them the scar on his chest, or bringing in his medical records or the newspaper articles about his kidnapping and attempted murder. But it wasn't worth it. They could see it if they read his Facebook page, but he hadn't wanted to friend most of them. And few of them had tried. No one had cared enough to even do a Google search about him, which would have confirmed his story. But even if they learned it was true, they'd just find something else to ride him about.

He'd gotten off to a bad start when word

got around that he was the infamous Emily Covington's brother. Her reputation had a way of keeping the gossip mill churning.

When Lance mentioned to a teacher in front of a class that he'd been shot in the lung last fall, word spread like wildfire that he wove these outlandish tales because he was jealous of his sister's notoriety. He'd become the class joke. Every effort he'd made to prove the truth only made him seem more delusional. Eventually he'd quit defending himself.

Only April, who marched to a different rhythm, had given him the time of day. But that wasn't so bad, because April was a cute misfit. He stayed awake nights plotting how to cross the threshold from friendship to romance with her. If he could get up the nerve, he planned to ask her to homecoming.

"Come on, Mr. Spock," she said, taking his hand and pulling him up. "Tell me about the fire."

Feeling better, he got his backpack and followed her out.

CHAPTER 13

Emily found a quiet place at the library and pulled her laptop out to study. Before she loaded her notes, she signed onto Facebook. After what had happened to her today, she wanted to talk to her friends. Her page was private, and her friends were real people she knew — not the strangers who tried to friend her every day. Most of those who had access to her wall were recovering addicts themselves, some that she'd made friends with in treatment, some through AA, and some were graduates of Haven House, the program she worked for. The bomb would freak them out, but they'd be able to relate to her mother's paranoia about a relapse. The people in their lives watched them constantly and blamed them for every negative thing that happened.

She logged on to Facebook and saw that several of her friends were also online. She clicked on her friend Sara, whom she'd met at Haven House, and sent her an instant message.

You won't believe what happened to me this morning.

Instead of taking the bait, Sara's instant message came up. *Did you hear about Bo's wife?*

Emily frowned. She only knew one Bo. He, too, had been a resident at Haven House while Sara was there, but they'd both been out of treatment for several months.

No, what about her?

Sara's answer came back quickly. *She was murdered in her bed this morning!*

Emily sucked in a gasp and slid back from the computer, staring at the IM. Murdered? Bo's wife was dead?

She thought of those two little kids that Devon had brought to Haven House to visit him on Saturdays. One was just a baby, the other a preschooler.

Check out this article, Sara said.

Emily clicked on the link, and it took her to the *Atlanta Journal Constitution's* website. The article had been posted online only an hour ago — "Atlanta Woman Found Murdered."

Devon Lawrence, 30, was found dead in her home this morning after an apparent

76

break-in and robbery. Her four-year-old child discovered her body. Devon's husband, William (Bo) Lawrence, 43, was notified at work at the JR's 24/7 on Broad Street. "It looks like someone came in the side door to the carport," he said. Several items were stolen from the home. Their 46-inch flat-panel TV was left untouched, however.

Emily brought her hand to her mouth, unable to breathe. Poor Bo. His wife murdered . . . her little girl discovering her . . .

He must be in shock.

A memory assaulted her. Emily's mouth went dry, and she looked around, making sure no one was reading over her shoulder. Her thoughts flew back to an afternoon she'd been working at Haven House, when Bo had talked about his wife.

But surely he hadn't meant the things he'd said.

They'd been watching that Hitchcock movie, *Strangers on a Train,* in the common room. It was a slow day, since some residents had broken rules and the whole group had lost their visiting-day privilege. Since she didn't have to check visitors in and out, she'd watched the movie with them from her desk, separated from the common area by a counter.

In the black-and-white thriller, two strangers meet on a train and get into a conversation about the people in their lives who've wronged them — a promiscuous wife and an overbearing father. The Robert Walker character, Bruno, says he'd like to kill his father, but he'd never get away with it. His obvious motive would point police to him.

Then he gets starry-eyed, and tells the other man of an idea he once had.

"Two fellows meet accidentally, like you and me. No connection between them at all, never saw each other before. Each one has somebody that he'd like to get rid of, so they swap murders. Then there's nothing to connect them. Each one has murdered a total stranger. Like, you do my murder, I do yours For example, your wife, my father. Criss-cross."

By the end of the movie, all the residents had gone out to smoke, except for Emily, Bo, and Carter. They'd laughed about the runaway merry-go-round at the climax of the flick, and Hitchcock's trademark cameo appearance.

Their conversation went back to the murdered wife and how she deserved what she had gotten. Then Bo had made the comment that, until now, Emily hadn't given much thought. "It is a solution, you know.

If it weren't for my wife, I could do what I want. I can't divorce her because she'd take the kids."

No, he hadn't meant it. He'd just been blowing off steam. Hadn't he?

From there, Bo and Carter had begun trashing the women they'd once loved.

Then Bo had said, "We could do this. I could kill your wife, Carter, and you could kill Devon. Ain't nobody who'd figure it out. We wouldn't even be suspects. Think about it. We live so far apart. I've only met your wife on visiting days here, and we ain't said two words to each other. Nobody would suspect me if she was murdered. And you could make sure you had a rock-solid alibi, so they wouldn't suspect you."

Emily didn't find it funny. "Come on, guys."

Carter wasn't smiling. "She ruined my life. Called the police on me, had me arrested."

"Mine, too," Bo said. "I wouldn't be in here if it wasn't for her."

"You said yourself that you had drugs in the house, out in the open where the kids could get to them," Emily pointed out. "She did the right thing."

"But she started this whole thing. Judge sends me to rehab, and I'm stuck here for three months. Now I have a felony conviction, all because of her. Divorce is no good," Bo said again. "She'd bring up my drug use and my arrests, and I'd be toast. She'd take the kids and I'd never see them. She'd poison their minds against me."

"Well," Emily said with a dismissive laugh, "then of course, you have to kill her." Shaking her head, she went around the counter and got the DVD out of the player. "They wouldn't let you watch this movie here if they knew it was giving you ideas. You guys are insane."

"It could work," Carter said to Bo. "It could actually work."

"Yeah," Bo said, chuckling. "But if we do it, we have to kill Emily, too. She knows too much."

Emily laughed as she went back to her desk. She understood rehab talk. People with too much time on their hands often fantasized about stupid things.

Bo stood up and looked at her over the counter. "Hey, Emily."

Emily turned back. "What?"

Bo was grinning. "We could take care of somebody for you, too. Got an ex-boyfriend you're sick of? Your mother, maybe?"

"No thanks. I don't sit around dreaming up murders. And the fact that you do tells me you need a lot longer than twelve weeks to get that kind of thinking out of your head."

When she'd gone home that night, she'd thought it was all a big, creepy joke.

But maybe it wasn't. Devon was really dead. And Emily knew too much.

Emily slammed her computer shut, as if that would make the situation go away.

What if Bo and Carter had gone from joking around to seriously plotting their wives' murders? And what if they were behind the bomb this morning? She was probably the only one who could link them to the crimes. It made sense that, if they were going to pull off these murders, they'd want to make sure she didn't talk.

Yes, it all made sense. It couldn't be a coincidence that some stranger had murdered Bo's wife the day a bomb was planted under Emily's car. She twisted her hair around her finger.

What about *Carter's* wife? Where did they live? She racked her brain, thinking. She'd met his wife a couple of times. She'd come from Birmingham to see him. Emily opened her computer, googled the Birmingham newspaper, and pulled up the obituaries. She typed Carter's last name, "Price," into the search box. Nothing came up.

It could be too soon. She went to the home page, scanned the list of articles posted today. Nothing about a woman being murdered in Birmingham. Maybe she was still alive.

Fear filtered through her. Carter's wife was in danger.

She grabbed her phone and punched in 911. Then she clicked it off. If she told the police, what would they do? This was out of Atlanta's jurisdiction. One of the crimes hadn't happened yet. How could she prove it?

Kent! She would tell him.

"Emily?" The girl's voice behind her made her jump, and she looked up to see a friend from her algebra class. "Are you okay?"

"Yeah. I was just studying."

"Didn't mean to scare you. You look awful."

She suddenly realized sweat was glistening on her face. "I'm fine. Just a little hot in here."

"Feels cold to me. They must spend a fortune on air conditioning."

Emily watched the girl walk away. She checked her watch. The test was in an hour. What was she going to do? She had to tell somebody about the murder plot. She couldn't just let this go.

She pulled out her phone and clicked on Kent's number. His voicemail came up. She thought of leaving a message, but the whole thing sounded too bizarre. She would wait until she could reach him and explain.

Quickly, she went back to Facebook, found Carter's page. She found his wife's name — Cassandra — but there was no phone number or address. She typed in White-Pages.com and entered "Carter Price." In seconds, she had a phone number and address.

Her heart pounded as she did a computer search for the phone number at the closest precinct to Carter's house in Birmingham. She wrote it on her hand, then packed her stuff back up. She couldn't make this call in the library, where everyone around her could hear.

Outside, she went around to the side of the building, set her backpack down, and made the call. Her hands shook as she keyed in the number.

"South Precinct."

Emily cleared her throat. "Uh . . . I'd like to report a crime. Or . . . a possible crime." She rubbed her forehead. "Is there a detective I could talk to?"

"Ma'am, if you have a crime to report, we could send a patrol officer to take your statement."

She paused as someone passed by, then when they were out of earshot, said, "No, I'm out of town. But I have to tell someone what I know."

She held while she was transferred to the Investigative Operations Bureau. A woman answered. "Detective Stone."

Suddenly Emily froze. She forced the words out. "Um . . . I asked the person who answered to connect me with a detective, because I have a crime to report."

"What's your name, ma'am?"

She knew they wouldn't take her seriously if she did this anonymously. "Emily Covington. I live in Atlanta." She hoped the detective didn't recognize her name. "I'd appreciate it if my name were kept out of this. Someone planted a bomb under my car this morning and I think it might be related to this."

"A bomb? Did you report it to police?"

"Yes, I did." She let out a breath. "But that's not the crime I want to report. See, I work at this drug rehab on Saturdays . . ."

"Okay," the woman said, impatience flattening her tone.

Emily closed her eyes. She was getting this all out of order. "No, wait. First, I have to tell you that there was a murder here in

Atlanta this morning. A guy I know who was a resident at the rehab . . . it was his wife."

"That's not our jurisdiction. You should call —"

"No, just listen. I think someone in Birmingham is going to be murdered next."

Silence, then, "Go ahead. I'm listening."

"A few months ago when I was at work, some of the residents were watching *Strangers on a Train*. Have you seen that movie?"

Detective Stone sighed. "Ma'am, could you get to the point? What crime has been committed?"

She paced as she spoke. "The movie is part of this. It's about two guys who talk about swapping murders, right? One guy suggests that he'll kill the other guy's wife, if the other character will kill his father. So after we watched the movie, these two guys came up with this hare-brained scheme to kill each other's wives. I thought they were joking, but today I find out that one of the wives is dead."

There was a pause. "What's the name of the woman who's dead?"

"Devon Lawrence. But like I said, she was here in Atlanta. The other wife lives in Birmingham. I'm afraid she might be next. Her name is Cassandra Price, and her husband is Carter Price. I think he's going to kill his wife! Or . . . not him, but the other guy. The one whose wife is already dead. Bo Lawrence from Atlanta."

The woman was quiet again. Emily hoped she was taking notes. "Okay, so you think they're going to kill each other's wives. We have no jurisdiction over an Atlanta case, and nothing has happened here yet if I'm understanding you."

"Do you really want to wait until she's dead? She's a nice woman, but her husband has a drug history. He may not be thinking clearly. Isn't there something you can do?"

The woman didn't answer. "Ma'am, could you tell me how we can contact you?"

Emily hesitated. "I gave you my name, and my number is on your caller ID. Are you going to do anything about this or not?"

"I've taken down the information you've given me. I'll have someone patrol that area."

"The reason I asked for a detective is that I thought you might be able to go by and warn the wife. I thought you might be able to look into where Carter was when the Atlanta woman was murdered."

"Yes." There was a long pause again. What was she doing? Waving another detective to her desk to get a load of this insane story?

"Well, thank you for the information, Miss Covington. We'll follow up."

Hope flowered in her stomach. "Will you really? And you'll do it fast, since it could happen any time?"

"Ma'am, give me your contact information."

What were they going to do? Come pick her up? She wanted to hang up, but she knew they already had everything they would need to find her. She gave them her address and phone number, then hung up. What if the woman hadn't taken her seriously? The story was too confusing, too outrageous. What if they didn't act in time? What if Carter's wife wound up dead, and there was something Emily could have done about it?

But she already *had* done something. Still, she couldn't count on the Birmingham police. How did she know they would stop Carter and Bo?

And the bomb . . .

Would Bo have taken the time to plant the bomb, letting his own children find their mother's body? Or had it been Carter? Carter only lived two hours away.

If Emily called and warned Carter's wife, what would Carter do? Maybe he'd realize it was too late and get cold feet, knowing that any attempts on his wife's life would be traced back to him. It might save this woman's life. But then he and Bo might come after Emily with a vengeance.

This whole thing was ludicrous. Was it even possible that these men who seemed to like Emily would want to kill her now? Yes, they were addicts, but they'd seemed like good guys when they were sober.

But there was no guarantee they'd *stayed* sober. In fact, they probably hadn't.

She closed her eyes. This was a test, she thought, even bigger than her sobriety. This test demanded that she do the right thing.

She tried calling Kent again. For the second time, his voicemail kicked in. Tears sprang to her eyes, and she waited for the beep. "Kent, this is Emily. Please call me. I might know who planted the bomb." She paused, then said, "It's a guy in Birmingham named Carter Price. I just talked to the police there. Call me and I'll tell you everything."

She hung up and thought of calling her mother. She checked her watch. Her mom would be setting up for the presentation by now, and she was probably already welcoming the church people in. She didn't want to mess her up again, not on such an important day. Her mother had lost her entire business because of all the emergencies that drew her away when Emily was using. Now she had a second chance at a job she loved, and this was the account that would give her job security for several years, if they won the bid.

Besides, she'd insist that Emily just sit still and do nothing. And Carter's wife could die.

Emily's heart raced as she sat on the steps next to the side door of the library. Maybe if she just called Cassandra and talked to her for a minute, warned her what had happened, she could save her life. But what if Carter answered?

If he did, she would tell him that she was letting him know about Bo's wife. Maybe somehow she could convey to him, without saying it, that she knew what he was up to.

Not allowing herself any more time to think it through, she called the number.

It rang once, twice . . .

. . . three times . . . four . . .

Finally the voicemail clicked on. It was Cassandra's soft, southern voice. "We're not here right now, but leave a message."

Now what? Should she leave a message? It was better than nothing.

Emily waited for the beep, cleared her throat. "Uh . . . Cassandra, I'm calling to warn you that something bad might happen to you. I think your husband is planning to have you killed. I know this sounds freaky, but please get out of town, and don't trust anybody." She hung up, willing her heart to stop hammering against her sternum.

No, she should have said more. Why couldn't she think better on her feet?

Unbidden, that old familiar craving roared up inside, making her long for something to calm her nerves.

Quickly, she snatched the thought back. No, she wouldn't let her mind go there. She wasn't in bondage to drugs anymore. They muddled her thoughts, loosened her inhibitions. They'd almost destroyed her life.

She was a new person. But she was still carrying that old Emily on her back. No matter what she did, she couldn't shake it off entirely. But she couldn't be deterred by her cravings or her pain. Cassandra Price's life might depend on her.

She shoved the laptop into her backpack. She'd have to bail on the test. She headed to the parking lot and got in her mother's car. She started it, then realized she had to at least call Dr. Ingles.

Like everyone else she'd called today, his recorded voice answered. She waited for the beep. "Dr. Ingles, this is Emily Covington. I wanted to let you know that something has come up about what happened this morning, and I have to go take care of it. I'm not going to be able to take the test at noon. I hope you'll give me another chance." Her voice broke. "I'm really sorry, Dr. Ingles. I'll talk to you later."

She hung up and wiped her face, knowing her professor wouldn't believe her. He would think she just wasn't prepared, that she was giving him a creative load of bull, a step up from *my dog ate my homework* or *my grandmother died.*

It didn't matter. This wasn't about her. She had to put Cassandra first. She had to go to Birmingham and save Cassandra's life.

CHAPTER 14

To Lance, the school cafeteria was a smorgasbord of anxiety. He walked into it each day full of dread, unless he saw April saving a place for him. Then he breathed out ten pounds of relief, hopeful that he could survive the half hour.

Today he didn't know if she planned to eat. She'd been depressed about problems between her parents and claimed she had no appetite most of the time. He looked around at the cliques sitting together — the proverbial popular girls hunched in gossip circles, the jocks nearby trying to get their attention, the weedheads munching with groggy eyes, the misfits huddled defensively together or scattered on the edges of the other groups.

Though he used to be a jock at his old school and had never given that status a second thought, Lance figured he fit the misfits most closely now. Funny how one move could change your whole life.

But he hoped he hadn't been quite as oblivious in Jeff City. His youth group at church had breached some of those walls, so he'd been friends with people from every group. At least, he thought he had. But maybe he just hadn't noticed the ones in pain on the outskirts of the crowd, longing for a place to belong.

The church they had chosen here was smaller, with a youth group that wasn't as close. So the class warfare carried into it, too, making him less drawn to it.

Gratitude relaxed him as he saw a hand waving over the crowd, trying to get his attention. April, saving him a seat. He waved and got his tray, then went toward her, his eyes on the seat next to her. But before he could get there, a bad-news dude named Tyson took the seat.

Lance's stomach sank. Tyson was one of those people who should have graduated from high school two years ago, but petty things like jail kept getting in his way. He could have taken his GED and been done with it, but Lance suspected he was here because the school was a prime drug market, and Tyson considered himself an entrepreneur. Lance thought of sitting somewhere else, but he couldn't leave April to

Tyson's fake charm. He took the seat across from her. "Hey, what's up?"

April smiled. "Nothing. Are you okay after this morning?"

Lance glanced at Tyson as he opened his milk carton. "Yeah, fine." He hoped his brevity would be a signal to April that he didn't want to talk about it in front of Tyson.

Tyson seized the moment. "What happened this morning?"

"Nothing," Lance said before April could answer. He racked his brain for a change of subject. "So . . . how are things with your parents?"

April's parents had been fighting and threatening divorce for weeks now, and it was an ongoing source of tension in her life. "Bad. Getting worse every day. They're sleeping in separate rooms, won't speak to each other."

"That's better than fighting," Tyson said flippantly.

"Actually, it isn't," April said. "I can't stand the silence."

"I love it when my folks aren't speaking," Tyson said. "It's bliss."

Lance couldn't imagine why Tyson was here, sitting with April. She wasn't anything like his friends.

"So . . . you want to hang out tonight?" she asked Lance.

He smiled. "Maybe. Can you get the car?"

Her smile faded, and she looked down at her French fries. "I don't know. It depends on my mom's mood. I doubt it."

He shrugged and bit into his roll, the only thing edible on his plate. "I doubt I can get my mom's. After this morning, she and my sister are having to share. I'll have to see what's going on."

"What happened this morning?" Tyson said again.

This time, April blurted it out. "Somebody put a bomb under his sister's car today."

Lance had told her to keep it quiet, but April could never keep a secret. "April, come on. I didn't want that broadcast."

"It was a secret?" she asked.

"Yes! I told you not to tell."

She winced. "I'm sorry, I forgot. I have a lot on my mind."

"Yeah, me too."

Now he had Tyson's attention. "A bomb? What happened, man?"

"Nothing," Lance said. "Just a little fire, that's all."

"She said a bomb. Somebody actually put a bomb there? What kind of bomb?"

"I don't know," Lance bit out. "I really

don't want to talk about it."

"Your sister," Tyson said. "She's the girl who was with that interventionist woman, right?"

Lance stopped chewing.

"Dude," Tyson said with a chuckle. "Sounds like that party girl's been hanging with some rough dudes again."

"Don't talk about my sister."

Tyson threw up his hands. "Hey, I just know how things work."

"She's fine," Lance said. "End of story."

"Sorry, dude. Didn't mean to offend."

"Let's change the subject," April said to Tyson. "I shouldn't have said anything."

Lance didn't look at her.

"Hey, listen," Tyson said. "I have a car. I can pick you up tonight and we can hang out."

Lance glanced up. He didn't like the way April's face lit up.

"Okay," she said. "You in, Lance?"

No way was Lance going anywhere with a drug dealer. "No. I probably won't go."

April didn't follow his lead. "Well, I'll go with you, Tyson. Pick me up at 6:30."

Tyson leaned in, flirtatiously close. "Okay. I've been trying to get you alone for weeks anyway."

April blushed, and alarms clanged in

Lance's head. He couldn't leave her to fend for herself with this jerk. "Changed my mind," he said. "I'm going. Pick me up, too?"

Tyson didn't seem put off. "Sure, Lance." He shoved him a napkin. "Give me your address and I'll be there. Your phone number, too, in case something comes up."

Lance knew what would come up. Tyson would "forget" him so he could be alone with April. But maybe April would insist. He wrote down his address and number.

"Text me if you have any more emergencies," Tyson said, jotting his number on another napkin. He winked at April. "See you tonight."

"No, I'll see you in chemistry."

"No way. I've had enough school today. I'm outa here."

Lance watched Tyson strut away, wondering why the school didn't expel him. He shot April a look. "What are you doing?"

She looked oblivious. "What? I didn't want to be rude."

"That guy is bad news. He's a dealer."

"Just because he's been to jail doesn't mean he deals. People can change."

"But he *hasn't* changed. He's high half the time in class, and he's selling to half the kids here. Ask anybody."

97

"That's just gossip. I don't go by gossip. If I did, I wouldn't hang out with you."

Lance felt his ears burning, and he looked back down at his food.

"Why did you say you'd go if you don't trust him?" she asked.

"Because I don't want you alone with him." There. He'd said it. "He's dangerous. You can't trust him. And if he's high when he picks us up, neither of us are going."

"You don't have to be a hero, Lance. I can handle myself."

"I'm still coming," he said.

"Good. But don't pick a fight with him. I don't want trouble."

Lance brooded as he swallowed the last of his roll, then choked down a suspicious-looking hamburger patty. He watched Tyson stop at each table. Some of the cliques treated him like a rock star instead of a criminal.

But Lance had known way too many people like him. Someone had to protect April.

CHAPTER 15

So far, the leadership of Three Roads Baptist Church seemed to like the ideas Barbara and the architects had for the sanctuary their congregation had voted to build. Paul and Martin Nelson, the brothers who owned the architectural firm, were pros at presenting plans, and they always left Barbara awestruck and inspired. It was a tough act to follow, but she'd learned long ago that it was the dressing on those plans that closed the sale. And that was her job.

The church leaders had been properly fed and seemed entertained as they listened to Paul and Martin's proposals. Barbara prayed silently that, in spite of what had happened with Emily's car that morning, she could focus on her part of the presentation.

She took her cue and went to the front of the conference room. "Well, ladies and gentlemen, now that you've seen the plan, you might be wondering about the finer points. So I've done some renderings here to show you what we're thinking. I have to tell you that designing a beautiful, glorious sanctuary like this, one that honors God and aids in worship, is the highlight of my career."

She pulled out the design board with all the fabrics, carpet samples, paint swatches, and furnishings, right down to the stained glass windows she hoped to commission for them. As she went through the renderings of what their church would look like, she gauged their reactions. They seemed captivated.

When the presentation was over, Barbara stayed to answer questions and allow the clients to touch the fabrics and offer input about the colors. By the time they left, she felt pretty sure that her firm would get this account. Paul attended the church, so he had inside knowledge of their needs. The other architects bidding on the job didn't have that edge.

"Great job, Barbara," Martin said as they gathered up their things. "You answered their questions beautifully. I liked how you emphasized that they would have plenty of input in choosing the interiors. I think we've got it in the bag."

"I hope so. Sorry again that I wasn't here for the meeting this morning, but it all worked out."

"Yeah. Hope everything is all right with Emily's car."

Now she hurried back to her office to see if she'd gotten a call from the police or her daughter. She had left her cell phone in her purse at her desk. A quick check revealed that Emily had called. She hadn't left a message.

Barbara picked up the phone and called her back. It rang three times before Emily answered.

"Hello?"

"Emily, I'm out of the presentation. Have you heard anything from the police?"

"No, not yet." Emily sounded distant, distracted.

"How did your test go?"

There was a long pause. "Um . . . I didn't take it yet."

"Why not? I thought it was at noon."

"I asked him if I could take it later. I was a little distracted by all this."

"And he said yes?"

Emily hesitated again. "I haven't heard back from him yet."

Barbara sank into her chair. "Honey, you just didn't show up? What if he doesn't give you another chance?"

"He will. He has to."

Barbara closed her eyes. "Look, I was distracted, too, but I did what I had to do. Emily, this is important!"

"I know, Mom!" she said. "Don't you think I know that?"

Emily was getting emotional. Barbara decided to back off. "Okay, just . . . call him again if you don't hear from him. Meanwhile, I'm going to call the insurance company and place a claim. Do you have the police report?"

Again, a hesitation. "Yes, but I can't bring it to you right now."

"Is there somewhere you could fax it to me?"

"No. I'm kind of tied up right now."

Barbara sighed. "Emily, I'm going to need that. Hopefully, they'll pay for a rental car so we won't have to keep sharing a car."

"I'll bring it when I can, Mom."

She sighed. "All right. Can you text me the number on the police report?"

"What number?"

"There's an incident number. It's probably at the top somewhere. Can you look?"

"Not right now. It's in my backpack, and I can't get to it. Mom, I have to go. I'll text it when I can."

"Hurry. I *have* to contact the insurance company."

"Okay, as soon as I can. 'Bye."

Emily hung up, and Barbara sat holding her cell phone, fighting the frustration rippling through her. Those old fears rose up in her again. Emily had sounded evasive, as she always had during her drug days.

But things had changed. This was not the old, drug-dazed Emily. She was different now. She just had a lot on her mind, she told herself, and she probably had a class to get to. Barbara clicked her phone off and put it back in her purse. She would just have to wait for that text.

CHAPTER 16

Emily hated withholding the truth from her mother, but she knew what would happen if she spilled out the whole truth over the phone. It would scare her mom to death, and she would tell Emily to stop and let the police handle it.

But a woman's life was at stake. Emily didn't want her to die, and the police might not do anything until a crime had been committed.

Her mother's car had a GPS system, so when Emily got to Birmingham, she pulled over and typed Carter's address in. She didn't know what she would do when she got there. What if Carter was home? What if Cassandra wasn't?

What if she was already dead?

Emily followed the GPS voice to the area where Carter lived. It wasn't as nice as where Emily's family lived. Carter's drug abuse had exiled him to an old run-down neighborhood, where there were as many boarded-up, condemned homes as there were houses that were occupied. She drove down Carter's street, looking for number 9340 on the rusted mailboxes. When she found it, there was no car in the open carport.

Maybe they only had one, and Carter was at his welding job.

She knocked on the door hard enough to shake the whole structure. As she waited, she rehearsed what she would say. *Cassandra, I'm so glad I found you. A woman is dead. You've got to get out of here. Your husband is going to have you murdered next.*

No, she couldn't say it like that. She'd have to give her more details to convince her to leave. She knocked again, listened, and heard nothing.

What now? Turning around, she looked up the street. Finally, she lowered to the front-porch steps. She could wait right here until Cassandra came home.

She'd sat there for a while when she noticed the neighbor next door peering out through her blinds. Emily lifted her hand in a wave. Eventually, the woman came out of her house and crossed the weed-spotted lawn. "Can I help you, hon?"

Emily got to her feet, swept her long hair

behind her ear. "Ma'am, is this the Price house?"

The woman offered her a toothless smile. "Sho' is. Who you lookin' for, baby?"

"Cassandra. Have you seen her today?"

"Yeah, she just left while ago."

Relief warmed through her. She was alive. "Had laundry baskets. Pro'ly went down to the laundrymat."

"Do you know which one she uses?"

"Fold N Fluff. Go down two stop signs, take a right, and it's up there on the right. I ain't swearin' she's there now, but she might be. She worked at the hospital the last three days, so she's pro'ly off today. Won't be rushin' home to work her shift."

Maybe she could catch Cassandra at the Laundromat and talk her out of returning home. "What about Carter? Is he at work?"

"S'pose to be, but you never know where that no-good scoundrel is. Pro'ly out smokin' crack somewhere."

That was what Emily feared, and it was the key to this whole thing. Relapse, insanity, violence . . .

She only hoped her being here was enough to stop the madness.

CHAPTER 17

Kent Harlan sat at his desk, studying the pictures he'd taken this morning of Devon Lawrence. There was something not quite right about the robbery that appeared to have cost the young mother her life.

"So what's hanging you up?" his partner Andy asked him.

"That flat-screen TV was left," Kent said. "I just don't get it. They took a couple of random things that weren't all that valuable — the jewelry she was wearing, even though the diamond in the engagement ring was small . . . the cash in her purse, which couldn't have been that much. Why wouldn't they have taken the TV or the computer?"

"Well, they may have been on foot, for one thing. Probably just escaped with what they could carry."

"So did he go there to kill her, or to rob her?" He studied the pictures again.

"Maybe he figured she wouldn't be there. When he found her home, he killed her."

"But her car was outside. The house didn't look empty. No, it looks premeditated. Somebody came in to find her. They made it look like a robbery. But they definitely knew she was there. And that sweet TV sitting on a cabinet. It's still sitting there. Just right for the games on Sunday."

"What are you thinking?"

Kent rubbed the lines between his eyebrows. "I don't know. The husband wouldn't want anything happening to his favorite toy. If he had something to do with it, he might have set it up to look like a robbery, but they only took things he didn't care about."

"He was at work. We have proof."

"Still could have had someone do it for him."

"He works at a convenience store. I doubt he makes enough to hire somebody to kill his wife."

"He has a bad drug history. Wife called the police on him a few months ago. He might have some resentments. Maybe somebody owed him money and did him a favor."

"Yeah, but there's no evidence he was dealing."

Kent felt the phone on his hip vibrating. He took it out of the pouch on his belt, saw

that Emily had called while he was interviewing a witness. He decided to call her
back on his landline, so he punched in her
number.

"Hello?"

"Hey, Emily. I saw that you called a while
ago. I've been working a case. Is everything
all right?"

He heard the strain in her voice. "Not
really. Did you get my message?"

"Not yet. What is it?"

"I heard something today that connected
some dots. Kent, have you heard about a
murder in Atlanta this morning? A girl
named Devon Lawrence?"

Kent sat up straighter. "That's the case
I'm working. Do you know her?"

"I've met her, when she came to visit her
husband at Haven House."

Of course, Kent thought. He hadn't even
asked Bo what rehab he'd been in, but it
was the common choice of most of the
judges in the area, since it was state-
supported.

"Kent, I think the person who killed her
might be the same one who put the bomb
under my car. Or if it wasn't him, he's connected to him."

"What? How do you know?"

"Because a few months ago I heard him

and another guy, Carter Price, talking about killing each other's wives."

Kent came out of his chair and motioned for Andy to pick up on the extension. It clicked as Andy got on. "Go ahead, I'm listening. Andy's listening, too."

"Sure, okay." Emily spilled out the story in a flood of detail. Kent took notes as fast as he could.

"Kent, you've got to do something about Cassandra Price. And check out where Carter was yesterday. I'm betting that either he or Bo planted the bomb, since I'm the only one who could connect them to the murders."

Kent rubbed the stubble on his jaw. "Did anyone else hear this conversation?"

"They may have, but I don't think so. There were people in and out. By the end of the movie, only Bo and Carter were left. I was the only one in the room when they said it. I'm the one they would be worried about. I would have told someone sooner, but I was sure they were joking around. I didn't even give it another thought until this morning."

"And you called the Birmingham police?"

"Yes, but this story sounds stupid. Some detective woman — Detective Stone — listened, but I doubt she took it seriously. If you could call her and let her know that this is serious, she might do something. I'm in Birmingham right now. I think Cassandra's still alive, but I'm trying to catch up to her and tell her what's going on."

Kent came to his feet. "You're in Birmingham? No, Emily. Get out of there. You can't be in the middle of this. Let the police handle it."

"But what if they aren't going to? What if they're just waiting for a crime to be committed?"

"I'll call them." He grabbed his notepad, turned the page. "Does your mother know you're there?"

She hesitated, then sighed. "No. I knew Mom would freak."

"She will, just like I am. Emily, I want you to turn your car around and go home. Now!"

"But what will it hurt to tell Cassandra to stay on guard?"

"You already did. You left a message on her voice mail, which was really not wise, Emily. What if Carter finds the message first? You're playing with fire."

"I had to do the right thing! I can't just go on with my day when I know that someone's about to be murdered! Besides, I tried calling you before I came."

"You should have filed a police report with Atlanta when I didn't call back right away, instead of going to Birmingham." He imagined what Barbara was going to say when she heard this. "Emily, come home now!"

She didn't answer.

"Emily? Do you hear me?"

Finally, a feeble reply. "Okay, I'm coming."

"Do not stop to talk to Cassandra. Do not go back to their house. Do not do *anything* except drive back to Atlanta. And when you get here, call me, because I need a formal statement from you."

"Okay."

"Call me when you get into town, and I'll meet you at your house."

"All right. But don't tell Mom, okay? She'll get all upset and think ridiculous things. I'll tell her everything when I get home."

Kent considered whether to keep it from Barbara or not. No, he couldn't lie to her if she asked. "Not promising anything, Emily. I'll meet you in two hours."

"Okay, but will you check out Carter Price and Bo Lawrence? See where they were when Devon was murdered?"

"Going to right now."

As he hung up, Kent glanced at his part-

112

ner. "Did you get that?"

Andy came back to his desk. "Yeah. You buying it?"

That irritated Kent. "Of course I am. I know this kid. She's not lying."

"Hey, I know her, too. I worked on her car with you. I remember her history."

"All drug-related. She's sober now, in college, doing great. We can trust her." But Emily's story sent the case to a whole new level. Now he wasn't just solving a murder as part of his job. Now he felt an urgency to protect the girl he already thought of as a daughter.

CHAPTER 18

Emily knew better than to buck Kent's orders, but still she pulled into the Fold N Fluff's parking lot to turn the car around. There were four cars there. One of them must be Cassandra's.

Through the window, she saw a woman at a washer. Yes, it was Cassandra. Emily could just go inside and tell Cassandra the whole story.

She sat in her idling car, watching Cassandra. She prayed that God would show her what to do. Should she do as Kent said, wasting the entire trip over here? Or should she just go in and make sure that Cassandra knew to keep her guard up?

Kent was looking out for Emily's best interests. But wasn't Christianity about putting others before yourself? She had to help Cassandra. She made up her mind as she shifted the car into park. She got out and went into the Laundromat.

The room hummed with rotating machines, and a steamy softness hung in the air with the scents of detergent and fabric softener. An old woman folded her laundry. A man sat in one of the orange vinyl chairs, texting.

And there was Cassandra, pulling wet laundry out of a washer. Emily stepped closer. "Cassandra?"

The woman spun around, startled.

"Sorry," Emily said, reaching out to calm her. "I'm Emily Covington. I met you when you came for visitation at Haven House."

The woman brought her hand to her chest. "Oh, yeah. I remember you."

"I knew your husband there. And I called you this morning. Did you get my message?"

Cassandra's face hardened, and she brought her eyebrows together. "You're the one who left that message?"

"Yes. I wanted you to know that I overheard —"

"Are you having a thing with my husband?" Cassandra cut in.

Emily caught her breath. "What? No!"

"I knew when I saw you that he was gonna get all fawny-eyed over you. With that long blonde hair, those eyes . . . You think I don't know what's going on?"

"No, Cassandra. You're wrong! That's not it!"

Cassandra grabbed her basket. Loading the wet clothes into it, she said, "Leave me alone. I don't know what you want from me."

"I want to save your life. I'm afraid Carter is going to do something . . ."

Cassandra slammed the washer shut, then headed for the door.

Emily didn't know what to do. "Cassandra, please listen. This is important. If you don't, you could die!"

But Cassandra shot out to her car, threw the basket in, and screeched out of the parking lot. Emily just stood there, stunned. She realized then that the others were staring at her.

"It's . . . she . . . I just had to tell her . . ." Why was she explaining to them? She pushed through the glass door and went back to the car.

Tears wet her face as she headed back to Atlanta. Kent was right. She had probably just made things worse.

CHAPTER 19

Barbara called the insurance company and tried to file the claim without the police report, since Emily still hadn't texted her the number. They took the information, but said they couldn't arrange for a rental car or an adjuster until they had all the details.

And now Emily wasn't answering the phone. Where was she? Would she remember to pick Barbara up from work?

She tried to stuff the fear back into its dark chamber at the back of her mind. Just because Emily had skipped the test didn't mean that she was up to anything. She had been doing well. The late nights weren't about drugs. They were just about a college kid testing her wings.

Weren't they?

Barbara felt weary. The weight of Emily's addictions were crushing her again. The signs were coming back. She didn't want to see them, yet she did. Maybe putting her trust in Emily again was wrong. Maybe she never should have let her guard down and given Emily so much freedom.

But she was a legal adult!

What would Barbara do if Emily dragged their family back into this again? Would she throw her out until she came to her senses? Would it come to that?

But hadn't she already come to her senses? She seemed sober. She appeared to be trying. Maybe this was all just delayed consequences of her past.

Barbara checked her watch. When did Emily have class on Mondays? She couldn't remember. Maybe she was in class and couldn't answer her phone. But she'd had plenty of time to call back.

She sat at her desk, staring into space. She should be celebrating. It looked as if they'd get the bid for the new sanctuary. But she couldn't think about victory right now. She could only think about failure.

She didn't even know if she *had* failed at helping Emily stay sober.

God knew what was going on. He knew what Emily was doing. He knew who had planted that bomb. She whispered a desperate plea for him to make things clear to her and help her face the truth.

But facing it might mean shaking the

foundation of their lives. She didn't know if she had the strength to deal with that again.

CHAPTER 20

The Avenger snorted another line of coke and waited as energy pumped through him. He hadn't slept in three days. He was living proof that sleep was a waste of time. With the proper fuel, he could go on and on. He wasn't like other mortals.

He pulled the page from the printer and studied the pill bottle label. It looked exactly like the one on the actual prescription bottle. He'd re-created it on the computer, Purdue Pharma logo and all, and put Emily Covington's name on it. Now he clipped the label out and glued it to the amber bottle full of Oxycontin. As he smoothed out the air bubbles, he laughed at the re-action Emily's mother would have when she found them.

He drove to the Covingtons' street, looking for any neighbors out working in their garden, walking the dog — anyone who might see and identify him. He saw no one, and he stopped at the end of the street, in front of a house for sale. Its yard was overgrown, so it was probably vacant. Perfect.

He took his bag, walked back to the Covingtons' house, and went around to the back door. He knocked, and when no one answered, slipped on his latex gloves and used a credit card to move the lock. He felt it disengage, then he pushed inside.

The Avenger stood in the kitchen, looking around at the granite countertops, shiny stainless-steel refrigerator, posh table and chairs a little too ornate for this size house. The mom was a decorator, and the house showed it. Elegant, his own mother would have called it, while she seethed with hatred for a woman who could pull this off.

A stack of yesterday's mail lay on the counter, most of it unopened. He unzipped his bag and pulled out the FedEx envelope he'd brought with the bottle inside. It had no fingerprints and no DNA. He'd worn gloves when handling it, and the seal was self-stick. He'd torn it open to make it look like Emily had already opened it. He set it on top of the mail.

But as he backed away, his appetite surged. Could he really leave a bottle of perfectly good Oxy lying there?

He went back to it, opened the bottle, shook out six pills. There were still twenty-four inside, enough to achieve his goal.

The drug called to him. He could easily grind it up and snort it or smoke it, or even shoot it. Maybe he shouldn't leave the bottle after all.

But then he stopped himself. He had plenty of crack at home, and that was his drug of choice anyway. And this was important. When pretty Emily's family found what was in that envelope, they would be hurt on so many levels. They'd never trust her again. Even better, if Emily found it herself, she might not be able to resist it. Slam dunk. She wouldn't be so full of herself then.

No matter who found the pills, he couldn't lose. If the Covingtons called the police about this break-in, they'd see the pills. Everything would go up in smoke for the smug do-gooder. He was a genius.

He wandered through the house, checking out the living room with its cushy sectional and upscale accessories. If his mother saw a room like this in one of her magazines, she would have torn the picture out and tacked it on the wall to dream about. It would have become another reason to churn with bitterness.

He went down the hall to Emily's bedroom. A four-poster bed dwarfed the room and crowded the huge dresser. A fancy gold jewelry box sat at the center of the dresser. He opened it and looked for the perfect piece.

There it was. A necklace with the letters EC hanging from a delicate chain. He took the necklace, pocketed it. He could use that later.

He found her makeup in the bathroom across the hall and grabbed a bright-red lipstick. Perfect.

Back in the kitchen, on the wall just inside the door from the garage — the one they probably used the most — the Avenger used the lipstick to write his message on the beige wall. He stood back and grinned.

This was too good not to brag about. He fished his phone out of his pocket, clicked on his camera, and took a picture. That would be worth a laugh later.

He looked around and figured enough damage had been done. Better leave now before the school bus dropped the kid off.

He smiled as he made his way back to his car, wishing he could be a fly on the wall to see what kind of chaos he'd given birth to.

CHAPTER 21

As if Lance's day hadn't been bad enough, now he was forced to ride the bus home because Emily wasn't answering his texts begging her to pick him up. With Emily's new problems, he doubted he would get his own car any time soon. He'd tried his best to save enough this summer to buy what his mom called "a reliable vehicle." He'd be content with a clunker as long as it ran. But her standard of "reliable" was stretching this thing out way too long. He'd managed to save a thousand dollars mowing lawns. Now he needed to find a part-time job so he could add to the till.

It was so unfair. Emily had gotten her car without putting in a dime. His mother claimed now that had been a mistake, that she was trying to build more character into him.

He didn't particularly want character. He just wanted a stinking car.

Emily would usually pick him up on Mondays, but not today. That meant he'd have to suffer the hour-long bus ride home. He was one of the last to be dropped off, so he had to sit there while each kid was taken home, one by one.

He got to the bus door, grabbed the chrome bar, and stepped inside. He'd hung back too long. It was almost full.

He glanced over the heads of the noisy students, looking for empty seats. One was next to a freshman. He headed toward it, meeting the eyes of some of his leering peers. As he came by, Jeff Samson stuck his foot out and tried to trip him. Lance stepped over it. "Nice try."

Big mistake, because the jerk behind him stuck *his* foot out then, and Lance stumbled over it. He pulled a Kramer and did a slapstick fall, going for laughs instead of mockery. Some of the kids giggled.

He made his way to the empty seat. The person by the window blocked it. "I'm saving this one."

Life was pretty lame when even the younger kids didn't want to be around you. Lance kept going, stepping over lanky legs, until he got to an empty double seat. It was in front of Brian Culpepper, who weighed three hundred pounds but was too slow for the football team. The kid was a bully on the bus, probably because others bullied him at school. Lance was his favorite target.

"Hey, Yankee boy."

Lance rolled his eyes. "Excuse me, but Missouri was part of the confederacy in the Civil War. Technically, I'm not a Yankee."

Lance doubted he even knew what the Civil War was. He unzipped his backpack and got out his iPod, shoved the ear buds into his ears.

Brian shoved him. "Are you disrespecting me, Yankee boy?"

Lance grabbed Brian's hand and sprang up, twisting his wrist around. "Keep your hands off me, dude."

Brian winced, and Lance let him go. The kid rubbed his wrist, looking embarrassed. Lance wanted to do more. He wanted to take that canned Coke in Brian's other hand and pour it over his head. He wanted to grab the bottom of Brian's shirt and pull it over his face. But the bus driver would freak out, and he'd wind up in detention.

Besides, Lance wasn't a bully. He didn't find the same joy in it that these over-sized toddlers did. He just wanted to be left alone.

CHAPTER 22

"I blame myself."

Bo Lawrence's words took Kent by surprise. They'd found him at his parents' house at 2:30, since his own was still a police-sealed crime scene. He'd been sleeping when they arrived, so they'd talked to his mother for a while before she woke him up. She reminded them that he had worked all night, only to learn that his wife had been murdered. She said he'd been with the kids since coming home from the police department and had fallen asleep with them when he put them to bed for a nap. "I worry about him," she said. "I don't want this to be his downfall after he's been doing so good, staying sober and all. It doesn't take much, you know, to trigger a relapse."

Now, Bo sat in his parents' living room, deep shadows hitting his face under the soft glow of a lamp. The curtains were drawn, blocking out the mid-afternoon sunlight.

He looked like a long-time drug user. His skin was dry, as though every drop of moisture had been sucked out, and wrinkles cut into his leathery skin as if he were much older than his early forties.

His eyes were bloodshot, but that could be easily explained by both fatigue and grief. It was hard to tell if he was sober or not. His pupils looked normal for the amount of light in the room.

"Why do you blame yourself?" Andy asked.

"Because . . . I know some shady characters. I've been racking my brain trying to think who's threatened me or had reason to get even."

"And?"

"And there are dozens." He pulled a paper out of his pocket, unfolded it with rough hands. "I made a list. Some of these dudes, I don't know their real names. They go by street names. People I cheated on some dope deals, a couple of guys I ratted out to the cops to get a better plea deal. I thought I was safe since so much time has gone by, but they might have killed her to get back at me."

Kent took the list, scanned it. Carter Price wasn't on it. "Did your wife have any enemies of her own?"

"I seriously doubt it. She was clean, trying to live right. Back when we met we partied all the time. She was as bad off as I was. But then she got pregnant with Allie, and she cleaned up. Never went back to it. I don't even know why she married me, because I was still in it."

The emotion on his face, the way the edges of his mouth pulled down, would have seemed genuine if Kent hadn't heard Emily's story. Bo stopped and pressed his thumb and forefinger against the outer corners of his eyes, hiding the tears that hovered there. They didn't seem fake, Kent thought as one rolled down Bo's cheek. If he'd been acting, wouldn't he have wanted them to see the tears, instead of hiding them? He studied the man — the way he sat slumped over, legs and arms open. It wasn't a posture of defensiveness or secrecy.

Maybe he was a good actor.

"You finished rehab a few months ago," Kent said in a soft voice. "Have you been sober since then?"

Bo seemed to pull back his tears, and dropped his hand. "Yes, but I ain't gonna lie to you. It hasn't been easy. I didn't even want to go to rehab. Didn't have any desire at all to change. But then when I got sober and saw all that I'd put my family through,

I kind of woke up one day, you know? Realized how much of my life I'd wasted. Got out of rehab, but I'm still on probation. Random drug tests keep me honest."

Kent tried to maintain a look of sympathy, hoping it would keep the man's guard down. He studied the list again, then brought his gaze back to Bo's face. "Bo, how well do you know a guy named Carter Price?"

There was a pause, and Bo frowned. "Knew him in rehab. We got to be pretty good buddies. He's a good guy."

"Have you heard from him since you got out of rehab?"

"A little, on Facebook, but I ain't been on there in a while. My Internet's messed up." He shifted on the couch, leaned forward, planting his elbows on his knees. "Why do you ask about him?"

"Do you remember watching a Hitchcock movie in rehab called *Strangers on a Train?*"

Bo's face changed, and he crossed his legs and brought his arms in. "Yeah, I remember."

"Do you remember a conversation you had with him about killing your wives?"

Bo's mouth slowly fell open. "What did he tell you?"

Kent could see that he'd hit a nerve. "So

130

you do remember that conversation?"

Bo stared at Kent for a moment as if constructing a reply. "We were kidding. You get bored in rehab, look for things to talk about. It was just a joke."

"Did he ever refer to it again after that night?"

"No, man." Bo opened his arms again, set both feet on the floor. "You don't seriously think he did it, do you? I mean, he knew I wasn't gonna kill his wife. Why would I do something that stupid, when I'm already in legal trouble up to my neck? We were joking!"

"Is it possible he didn't know that?"

"No! We never talked about it again, because we both knew it was a stupid joke. He ain't insane like that dude in the movie."

"So if we get your phone and email records, we're not gonna see communications between you and Carter?" Andy asked.

"No, man. None. Look, Carter was bad off when he came to rehab, and he wasn't real happy with his wife. But I don't think he had it in him to kill anybody."

"Even if he relapsed?"

"*Especially* if he relapsed. He was a weed-smoking Xanax addict. Those drugs made him lazy, man. No way he'd go to all that trouble to come over here and kill my wife.

131

What would be in it for him?"

"If he thought you'd kill his own wife, he might get up the energy."

"He knew I wouldn't. That's crazy." He got up, rubbing the back of his neck. "But find out where he was. I want to know."

"We intend to," Kent said. "Bo, were there any others who heard that conversation?"

Bo scratched his head. "Emily some-body . . . cute little chick who worked there. And maybe a couple of others were in and out. I don't really remember who was there with us when we had that conversation. But if you think this is a lead, man, you may be off on a rabbit trail. I want you to find Devon's killer, but I don't think it's Carter Price."

"Did you or Carter have anything against Emily?"

Bo gaped at him, as if he couldn't follow the direction of this conversation. "No, she was cool. She'd been in recovery herself, so she understood us. She didn't give us a hard time like some of the other staff members did." His face changed. "Is *she* the one who told you about that conversation?"

Kent didn't answer.

"Yeah, that makes sense. When she saw that Devon was murdered, she probably

132

thought of that. I don't blame her. But she's wrong."

Back in their car, Andy looked at Kent. "So let's go to the station and pull Bo's phone records. Maybe Birmingham has finished interviewing Carter Price by now."

"It'll be interesting to see if he has an alibi for last night."

"You sure you didn't show Bo too many cards? Mentioning Emily?"

Kent shook his head. "I showed him just enough to keep him from killing Cassandra Price if he had a mind to do it. And hopefully it'll make him leave the Covingtons alone, too. If he communicates with Carter Price tonight, maybe they'll call the rest of the scheme off."

CHAPTER 23

When Emily finally texted Barbara the police report number at around three in the afternoon, Barbara was able to finish filing the claim on Emily's car. When they'd arranged for her to get a rental, she called Emily again. This time Emily answered.

"Hey, Mom." The rumble of her car engine muffled her voice.

"Emily, I've been trying to reach you all afternoon."

"I know, I'm sorry. I have a lot on my mind, so I forgot to text you the police report number till a few minutes ago."

"Yes, I got it. They're arranging for a rental car. You have to be twenty-one to drive it, so I'll drive the rental and you can use my car until we know what's going to happen with your car. But come pick me up now so we can go get it."

There was a long pause. "I can't right now."

"Why not?"

"Because I have class."

The moment the words were out of Emily's mouth, Barbara knew she was lying. She never had class after 3:00 on Mondays; she almost always picked Lance up. "What class?"

Emily sniffed. That sniff was a dead giveaway that she was lying. Since she was a little girl, Emily always sniffed before blurting out an untruth. "It's a lab. My professor called it at the last minute."

"A last-minute lab." It wasn't a question. Did Emily really think she was buying this? "Emily, where are you?"

Emily sighed. "Mom, I'll tell you everything when I get home, okay? I promise. Just . . . right now, I can't come get you."

"Then you *were* lying about the lab?"

No sniff this time. "Okay, yes. But I'm about an hour from home, so I can't get there. It's okay. Kent knows all about it."

Barbara frowned. "Kent? You've heard from him? Has he found out anything about the bomb?"

"No, not yet. But I called him because I thought of some things he needed to know."

Barbara's heart sank. Had Emily been forced to make a confession to him? Why hadn't he called her? Her chin set, she bit

135

out, "Emily, where are you?"

Finally, Emily blurted it out. "I went to Birmingham. I had to talk to somebody. But I'm on my way home, and everything is all right."

"*Birmingham?* That's two hours away. You don't know anybody in Birmingham."

"Yes, I do. From Haven House."

That agitated Barbara's fears. She brought her hand to her chest. "Emily, is this about drugs?"

"No, Mom, I promise it's not. Please, just calm down. I have a lot to tell you, but my phone is about to die and I don't have the charger. I'll tell you everything as soon as I get home." Before Barbara could demand more, Emily cut the call off.

Barbara dropped the phone and sat back hard in her chair. What was happening? A bomb, her daughter's skipping a test, a sudden trip to Birmingham to see somebody she'd met at a drug rehab?

"Barbara? Are you all right?" Barbara's assistant, Lena, stood in the doorway.

"No . . . yes."

"I thought the presentation went well. Didn't you get the account?"

Barbara tried to draw in a breath, but her lungs couldn't seem to hold it. "We haven't heard yet. I just . . . I'm tired." She shook her head to redirect her thoughts. "Listen, could you drive me over to the car rental place? I have to pick up a car."

"Sure. I'll get my purse."

Barbara tried to focus as she got her purse and glanced around her desk. What should she bring home? Her purse, her briefcase, her cell phone . . .

On the ride over, she could hardly put two thoughts together. Lena chattered about some of the office gossip, but hardly any of it registered.

The car was ready when Barbara went in, and she left quickly. Instead of going back to work, she headed home to wait for Emily.

As she drove into her neighborhood, Barbara glanced around for anyone who might not belong there . . . someone who might be capable of planting a bomb. She saw nothing unusual. She pulled into her driveway, clicked the garage door opener. The charred place on the driveway was still there, reminding her that someone had been here during the night.

She didn't get out of her locked car until the garage door had closed behind her. Maybe she was just being paranoid. It had probably just been some stupid kid who didn't even know who they were. He'd probably picked their house randomly.

She made her way into the kitchen, dropped her purse on the counter. She lowered to a bar stool, wishing she could relax. Her eye caught her reflection in a mirror on the wall. . . .

And then she saw it.

In red lipstick across the wall behind her . . .

She spun and saw the red letters.

Criss-Cross.

She let out a yelped scream. She grabbed her purse, almost dropping it as she dug for her cell phone.

"911, may I help you?"

"Yes, I need the police. Someone's broken into my house. It's 311 Crimson Drive."

"Ma'am, are they still in the house?"

Terror choked her, and she jerked around, looking toward the hall. "I . . . I don't think so. I don't know."

"Ma'am, get out of the house. Is there a neighbor you can go to, to wait for the officers?"

She grabbed her purse and went out the back door. "Yes. I'll do that. Please, tell them to hurry."

She crossed the backyard and hurried around to the front of the house. How had someone gotten in? There was no broken glass, no sign of forced entry that she could tell. She looked around, trying to decide where to go. She rounded the hedge separating her house from the couple next door, who were still at work. There were rocking chairs on their front porch. She would wait there.

While she did, she called Kent. He picked up on the second ring. "Hey, babe."

She didn't want to hear *babe.* Kent was keeping something from her. "Someone has broken into my house," she said. "The police are on their way."

He paused, and rage filled her heart. Without waiting for an answer, she spat out, "Where has Emily been, Kent? Why didn't you tell me she went to Birmingham?"

"Whoa, one thing at a time," he said. "How do you know someone broke in?"

"They wrote on my wall!" she shouted. "They were in my house! Who is this person? Is my daughter safe?"

Kent's pause was more than she could take. "I'm coming right over, Barbara. Where are you?"

"I'm on the next-door neighbor's porch waiting for the police to come for the second time today!"

"Good. Stay right there. I'll be there in a few minutes."

The phone cut off, and she stared at it, feeling completely helpless. She got up and paced across the lawn, watching her house. She heard a door open across the street and saw her nosy neighbor coming toward her. "Barbara!" she called.

Barbara braced herself as Kerry crossed the street. She was the only neighbor home during the day, and she was probably mining for gossip. "Hi, Kerry." She couldn't manage a smile.

"Barbara, strange things are happening over here today. What's going on?"

Barbara stared at the woman. "Why? Did you see someone over here?"

"The police," Kerry said. "This morning. Fire trucks and foam all over the place. And now you're standing on the Bennetts' porch."

"Oh. We had a little fire this morning. But did you see anyone here this afternoon?"

"No, why?"

"Because my house was broken into," Barbara said. Why was it that Kerry saw everything *she* did, but not a burglar breaking into her house?

"No, I didn't see anybody. I've been here all day. When did it happen?"

"I don't know," Barbara said.

"Well, what did they take?"

140

"I don't know yet," she repeated. "I'm waiting for the police."

Kerry touched her chest. "I knew it. When your family moved in, I knew we were going to have trouble."

Barbara's mouth fell open. "What are you talking about?"

"Your daughter." She said the word as though it were profane. "I saw all about her on the news a couple years ago. Now, I know everybody says she's doing better, but girls like her bring trouble wherever they go."

Barbara wanted to slap the woman. But how could she fault her for having the same feelings Barbara was having? "My daughter didn't break into our house," she said through her teeth. "She lives here."

"Don't be naive, Barbara. They steal to buy their drugs, and if they don't, their friends do. Did you check your pharmaceuticals? Maybe you just haven't noticed your drugs missing yet. I had a cousin whose son was on drugs, and he used to sell —"

Barbara stopped her. "Kerry, I appreciate your concern, but Emily is in college and doing great, and this has nothing to do with her." She wished she knew that for sure. "Now, if you'll excuse me, I have to make a phone call."

141

Barbara turned away and pretended to make a call. As Kerry crossed the street again, she didn't head home, but instead went to another neighbor's. The rumor mill would be active by sundown.

Barbara stood in the warm wind, hugging herself. She had to pull herself together.

And where was Emily? Why wouldn't she tell her on the phone what was going on? Why weren't the police here yet?

"Relapse is part of recovery," Emily's counselor had told her last year in family counseling. She'd wanted to scream that relapse was not an option, that she couldn't take any more, that she had to protect herself and her son. But many of the girls Emily knew from rehab had relapsed. Why did Barbara believe her daughter was immune?

So what was she going to do now? The secrets and lies were reminiscent of the past. How had this happened?

After a moment, two police cruisers pulled up to her curb, and she crossed the yard to meet them. She told them what she'd found, and they made her wait while they went into the house. As they went in, she heard the school bus turning onto their street.

It halted in front of their house, and she

heard the yells of the kids calling out the window at Lance and laughing like hyenas.

"Cool, police!" one of them shouted.

"What did you do, Covington?"

Lance got off and crossed the street in front of the bus. His face looked pale as he came into the yard. "What now?" he asked her.

She gave him a distracted hug. "Someone broke in."

He looked like he was going to be sick.

"Are you all right?" she asked.

"Yeah. Where's Emily?"

"On her way home. She went to Birmingham today for some inexplicable reason. I have no idea what's going on. Do you?"

He shrugged. "Yeah, I have an idea. This is looking a lot like two years ago."

"You think she's relapsed?"

"Don't you? Mom, these things don't just happen . . ."

One of the cops came back out of the house. "It's all clear. No one's there."

She breathed relief and saw Kent's car pulling into her driveway. He got out, a guarded look on his face. He came to hug her, but she pulled back, putting distance between them. "Kent, I want you to tell me what's going on right now."

"I just talked to Emily," he said. "She's

almost home. Just let me go in and talk to the officers. When she gets here, we'll sit down and talk."

Barbara couldn't accept that. "Kent, is this about drugs again? Has Emily been using?"

"I don't think so, Barbara. I'd tell you if I did." He kissed her cheek, but she stared coldly at him. Backing away, he went into the house, leaving Barbara and Lance in the yard with their imaginations.

Lance shrugged off his backpack, let it drop to the ground. "I can't believe this. I actually had plans for tonight. Now I probably can't go."

"What were your plans?"

"I was going to hang out with April."

Barbara felt for her son. His life had been as altered by Emily's choices as hers had been. It wasn't fair. "You can still go, honey."

"Not if our lives are crashing down around us again." He glanced up the street, saw Emily coming in Barbara's car. "There she is now."

Barbara stepped out to the curb as the car slowed. Emily carefully turned into the driveway and parked next to Kent's car. Barbara strained to see her through the window. What did she look like? Were her eyes red? Her pupils constricted like she was on opiates, or dilated like she was on benzos? Was she jittery like she was on cocaine?

As Emily got out, Barbara thought she looked normal. Sober. Her steps were straight, and she didn't wobble. Maybe she wasn't on anything. Barbara wanted to believe that, but rage burned in her heart.

Emily reached for her, but again, Barbara held herself back. "Was that message they left for you?"

Terror and dread narrowed Emily's eyes. "What message?"

"The one this person wrote on the wall after they broke into our house!"

Emily sucked in a breath.

"It said, *Criss-cross.* What does that mean, Emily?"

"Oh, no."

Barbara wanted to scream. "Emily, *who's* doing all this?"

"Let's go in and sit down." Emily's hands shook slightly, but more like she was nervous, not loaded. Not wanting to make a scene where neighbors could see, Barbara and Lance followed Emily in and pointed her to the wall.

Emily was silent as she stared at the message.

Kent met them in the kitchen. "They said there were no fingerprints. No broken lock. They don't know how he got in. Either he had a key, he picked the lock, or he used one of your garage door openers."

Barbara turned to Emily. "Did you notice if yours was in your car this morning?"

Emily swallowed. "No, I didn't notice." She drew in a long, deep breath, then cleared her throat. "Mom, Lance. Can you sit down? It's time to tell you everything."

CHAPTER 24

The cocaine high was beginning to wear off as the Avenger reached the outskirts of Birmingham. He pulled into a rest stop and went into the bathroom. Three days' fatigue threatened to crash in on him with agonizing urgency, but he couldn't let that happen. He didn't have any come-down drugs like Xanax with him to ease his crash.

Besides, he still had too much to do today. His genius superplan was only partially fulfilled. There was so much more havoc to be wreaked.

He lumbered back to his car, his limbs as heavy as lead. Not good. Time to use again. Thankfully, he had an ample supply, because he'd gotten access to his mother's bank account. He'd cleaned it out and spent it all on things that mattered.

He poured out another line of coke, snorted it, and waited for it to revive his body. He had to hurry. He had to get to

Cassandra before Carter got off work. The timing was essential.

He snorted a second line, then licked his fingers, unwilling to lose one grain of the fine powder.

Power and strength returned to his brain with a jolt.

Cassandra. He wished he'd gotten to know her the few times he'd seen her on visiting day at Haven House. Then she would trust him and let him in. As it stood, he'd have to do some finagling to get into her house. But he could do it.

He flew down I-20 to the exit. Music revved him on, pumping him with purpose. He found Carter's neighborhood, as run-down and sad as his own.

As he'd hoped, Cassandra's car sat in the double carport. She was home. Perfect.

He parked his car half a block down, in front of a house that looked like no one was home, stuffed his gun in the waistband of his jeans, and strode to her house.

Plan A was to ring the bell and see if she answered. When she opened the door to a .44 Magnum, he would have no trouble getting in. Once inside the house, he would crank up her stereo to maximum volume and muffle the gun with a pillow. If anyone heard the gunshot, the confusion of guitars and drumbeats might make them question what they'd heard.

At her door, he heard the sound of a television inside. He studied the doorknob. He could easily get in with a credit card if she didn't open it. And the door looked warped and hollow, easy to kick through if it came to that.

Showtime. He pulled his gun but kept it behind him in case she peeked out. He rang the bell.

"Who is it?" she called through the door.

"UPS," he said.

She opened the door then, peering out cautiously. He raised the gun and shoved the door open with his shoulder. She stumbled back, and he slammed the door behind him.

"You!" she said.

"Good to see you again, Cassandra. Sorry I can't stay long."

Chapter 25

At the kitchen table, as Emily finished her story about the viewing of *Strangers on a Train*, Kent's eyes settled on Barbara's face. The terror in her eyes reminded him of the first time he met her. Clearly, Emily's recounting of what she knew had pulled Barbara back into a maternal nightmare.

When she finished, Lance breathed out a humorless laugh. "I gotta see that flick."

Emily seemed to study Barbara — the glisten of fear in her mother's eyes, the dryness of her lips, the way she wiped her palms on her skirt. "I need for you to believe me," Emily said.

Barbara's hand trembled as she brought it to her face. "It's just . . . too outrageous to be made up."

Kent slid his chair back, walked into the dining room to the front window, and looked out. He couldn't escape the feeling that they were being watched, or listened to. The house wasn't safe. He'd have to get them out of here.

"You thought I'd relapsed," Emily said.

Barbara didn't speak for a moment, but Lance did. "You gotta admit, it was looking bad."

Kent went back to them. Barbara looked drained, wiped out. He wanted to go to her, comfort her, but her mind wasn't on him. She was locked in on Emily.

"What do they want?" she said. "Was that message threatening you? What does *Criss-Cross* mean?"

"It was just a line from the movie," Emily said, looking at Kent. "But why would they want to identify themselves? Even if I hadn't already thought of them, that message would have reminded me. It has to be either Bo or Carter."

"Bugs me, too," Kent said. "It's like signing their names. Something's not right."

"If they hadn't planted the bomb, I might have gone a long time without knowing about the murder," Emily said. "Now they're waving a flag. Daring me to talk."

"This is so dangerous," Barbara whispered, turning her glistening eyes up to Kent.

"And that poor woman, Cassandra," Emily said. "I tried. I approached her and tried to warn her. She accused me of having a thing for her husband. She wouldn't listen."

"So . . . if Devon is dead," Lance said, "then Carter would have done it. Maybe Carter is the one who planted the bomb, since it must have happened during the same hours that Devon was murdered and Bo was at work."

"Had to be," Emily said.

"So today, would it be Bo or Carter who broke in?" Barbara asked.

"I don't think it could have been Bo," Kent said. "I was questioning him most of the morning. Then I went by his parents' house to ask him more questions this afternoon at about 2:30. His mother said he'd been with his kids at her house since leaving the police station. She could be covering for him, but I have pretty good instincts, and she seemed sincere. The Birmingham police are looking for Carter. They're going to question him about all this. Meanwhile, I want you all to get out of here."

Barbara stood up, strength hardening her face. "We'll go to a hotel."

"You could stay at my place," Kent countered. "And I could stay here and watch your house. Might be able to catch them if they come back."

She slammed her hand on the table. "No,

Kent. I don't want you here, either."

"Barb, it's my job. It's part of a case. This guy has to be stopped, and he's getting sloppy. You and the kids can get some rest at my house, and he won't know to look for you there."

"But he could kill you."

"I'm armed. This is what I do."

She stared at him, and he slid his hand into his pocket and felt the ring. "I don't want two people I love in danger," she said.

The words sent a warmth through him. He slipped the tip of his finger into the ring, then dropped it to the bottom of his pocket. "Barbara, I'll be okay. I don't want you to worry."

But she would. He rarely told her about the dangers he entered into weekly, if not daily. The truth of his job strained relationships. His first wife couldn't take the stress. She'd left him for an accountant.

He took out his keys, pulled off his house key. "Here. The house isn't all that clean, but it'll do. You and Emily can take my bed, and Lance can have the guest room."

She took the key. "Are you sure?"

"Of course." He wanted to say that they were his family, but he restrained himself.

Emily looked back at her mother. "Mom, I'm sorry I lied to you today."

"Don't do it again, Emily. I understand why you did it, but it was dangerous and didn't accomplish anything." She let out a long, weary sigh. "I want this whole drug thing to be done, with no residue. It's infected our lives like toxic mold. We can't clean it off. We have to rip out all the sheet-rock and start over with the rafters to get rid of it."

Kent saw the sorrow on Emily's face, as if she thought she was the sheetrock . . . or the mold.

"I didn't *do* anything," Emily said. "I was just working. And those guys, they seemed okay. They seemed . . . nice. Not like people who could kill their wives. I never thought in a million years that they were serious. I thought they were just trying to get a rise out of me."

Kent glanced toward the kitchen, where that message still stained the wall. If the prowler had taken anything, they couldn't tell it yet. His eyes swept the counter. A stack of mail lay there. A FedEx envelope lay open next to the stack. An alarm went off in his head. Getting up as Emily went on, he stepped toward it, saw Emily's name on the air bill. He lifted up the open edge . . . and saw a bottle of pills.

His heart jolted. Most of Emily's drugs in

the early days of her addiction had come from online pharmacies. So what drug would she be getting in the mail?

Kent pulled the pills out.

Barbara turned at the shaking sound. "What's that?"

Kent set the bottle down. "Oxycontin. It has Emily's name on it."

Suddenly Emily shot to her feet, throwing her arms up in self-defense. "No way! I didn't order that stuff."

"Well, I sure didn't," Barbara said.

"Mom, do you honestly think that's mine — after everything I told you?"

Barbara went to the stack of mail. "Did you bring the mail in today? The rest of this is yesterday's." Barbara grabbed the envelope. "It's addressed to *you!*"

"I haven't even been back home today. I didn't bring this in." Emily picked up the bottle, read the label. It had her name on it, but it wasn't a pharmacy she had ever used. "Kent, I didn't do this. Maybe the guy who broke in left this to make it look like I'm using. If it was Bo or Carter . . . maybe they're getting some perverse pleasure out of making it look like I've relapsed. But I'll take a drug test right now. Test me."

Tears starting in her eyes, Barbara went for the bottle.

"No, don't touch it," Kent said. "I have to log it."

"Yes, take the bottle," Emily told Kent. "See if you can find fingerprints. Maybe they're his."

Kent hoped there was still something there. He bagged the bottle, then led the others around the house, looking for anything else the prowler may have left. They found nothing.

The doorbell rang, its chime sounding throughout the house. Everyone turned to Kent. "Go pack," he said. "I'll answer." He went to the door, peered out the small window. Two uniformed cops stood on the porch — the same ones who'd been here earlier. He opened the door. "Forget something?"

One of them wet his lips, as if he dreaded what he was going to say. "Kent, I know you're close to this family. But we have an arrest warrant for Emily Covington."

He heard the family coming up behind him. *"What?"* Barbara cried.

Kent held his hand up, as though he could shield them from this. But he dropped it to his side. "A warrant? What's it for?"

"For the murder of Cassandra Price in Birmingham."

Kent turned back to Emily as the officers stepped into the house. Her face was white.

CHAPTER 26

The police officers who had been there as protectors earlier were now Barbara's enemies. "Get your hands off my daughter!" she shouted as they tried to cuff Emily. "What is going on?"

"Hold it, guys," Kent said over her yelling. "I want to talk to the one who issued the warrant."

One of them gave him the arresting officer's name — Detective Stone, from Birmingham, whom Kent had already talked to once today.

Emily looked as if she might hit the floor. "She's dead?" she asked, face twisted. "He killed her? I tried to tell them. I tried to warn her!"

"Sit down, Emily," Kent said, punching out the number on his phone. "Everybody just calm down. Guys, just give me a minute."

But Barbara couldn't calm down. "How

can they think she did this, when she's the one who's been waving a flag all day long? Did they tell you that? Do you even care?"

Kent waited as the phone rang at the Birmingham police department. "Barb, it's not their decision to make. They're just doing their job."

"Don't defend them!" she cried. "This is insane, and we're supposed to accept it because there's a warrant?"

Someone answered for the BPD, and Kent asked to be transferred to Detective Stone. Finally, she picked up. "Detective Stone, Kent Harlan again. I understand you've issued a warrant for Emily Covington."

"That's right. Have your people brought her in yet?"

"We have her here." All five people in Barbara's living room gaped at him, hanging on every word, so he opened the door and stepped out onto the front doorstep. "Tell me about Cassandra Price."

"Her neighbor found her an hour ago," Stone said. "Shot through the head in her living room."

He closed his eyes. "Just like Emily predicted. Why is she a suspect?"

"Because there was a necklace with the initials EC found on the floor a few feet from the body."

His heart crashed.

"It had her fingerprints on it. And she was stalking Cassandra today."

"Stalking?"

"Yeah. Cassandra Price called the police department twice today. The first time she reported that a woman left a message on her machine telling her that she was going to die. That call came from Emily Covington. Later, Price reported that Emily approached her. The neighbor who found the body identified Emily as the woman she talked to at the Price house earlier today."

Kent forced back the urge to defend Emily. He had to be professional. "I'm aware of that. According to her statement, Emily wasn't threatening her, she was *warning* her. Did you check Cassandra's husband's whereabouts?"

"He was at work. He works at the steel plant, and all the people on his shift were able to vouch for him."

Kent heard Barbara's angry voice on the other side of the door. He hoped she didn't get arrested, too. "You guys must have something on the DA if he gave you a warrant with this little evidence."

Stone didn't appreciate that. "That isn't helpful, Detective Harlan."

He rubbed his eyes. "What was her time

160

of death?"

"The case is still new, and we haven't gotten a time of death yet. But it happened sometime between 2:30 and 4:30. She was discovered just before 5:00."

Kent tried to think. If the murder scheme had been carried out, Bo would have been tasked with Cassandra's murder. But his mother said he'd been with her and the kids all day. Kent had been with him around 2:30 to 3:00. It was a stretch to think Bo could have made it to Birmingham within that timeframe. But if he'd flown over the speed limit, it was possible.

"I've been interviewing Emily since she got back to Atlanta at 4:30. She left Birmingham just after 2:30."

He rubbed the bridge of his nose and tried to think. A necklace at the scene? Emily did often wear a necklace like that, but she hadn't been wearing it today. He'd noticed this morning because she'd been wearing the cross necklace that he'd given her for her birthday — the one she was wearing now. "Listen, I can't help wondering about this necklace. It's just too convenient . . . her leaving evidence with her initials behind. She's been in contact with the police like four times today. She called you this morning, and she told me exactly what she's been doing. That's not the MO of someone who'd just committed murder, or *planned* to commit murder. If her story is true, then Bo Lawrence would have been the one who'd want Cassandra dead."

"You just said he has an alibi."

Kent wiped a drip of sweat from his temple.

"This story Emily Covington is telling," the detective said. "It's pretty *out there,* don't you think?"

He tried to control his voice. "Why would she call our attention to herself if she was the killer? If she'd just kept her mouth shut we never would have connected her. Even the necklace probably wouldn't have led you to her."

"Maybe she's playing a game. Drugs do bad things to people, Detective. I don't have to tell you that."

Kent didn't want to tell her that he knew Emily, that he'd seen her spiritual growth, that he hoped she'd be his daughter soon, that she wasn't on drugs. "There was an attempt on her life this morning, too. Somebody planted a bomb under her car, then later there was a break-in at her home. The necklace must have been stolen then."

"She could have set that up herself to make herself look like a victim."

162

He wanted to kick something. "But she didn't even notice it was missing! Everything's a possibility, but it has to make sense. We can't just dismiss her story."

"I agree with you," Stone said. "Why don't you drive over tomorrow and we can put our heads together? I assume they'll transport her tonight?"

Kent glanced back at Barbara's front door, trying to think. Somehow, he had to delay her transport. "No, I can't let her go. If she's a suspect in the Price murder, then I have to question her further about the Lawrence case here."

The woman gave a disgusted sigh. "All right, Detective, but do it tonight."

Kent's head was throbbing by the time he got off the phone.

CHAPTER 27

Emily tried to hold back the tears as Kent intervened for her, telling the arresting officers that he would transport her in and that she didn't require handcuffs. At least the neighbors wouldn't see her being marched to a police car like a lowlife criminal.

Her mother was hysterical, yelling at the cops as if *they'd* killed Cassandra Price and pinned it on Emily.

She tried to think. If Bo was with his mother and children all afternoon, as Kent believed, then Carter had to have done this. Surely when they found Cassandra dead, they'd checked on him first. She thought of the man with leathery skin who looked much older than he was. He'd been skinny and small, not the violent kind. But when someone was in active addiction to a drug, their body screamed out for more. And if they couldn't get it, they were unpredictable, and anyone who got in their way could be in danger.

But this had been murder, calculated and deliberate, not a crime of passion committed because Carter had lost his temper or craved drugs. And why would he have taken the time to drive here and plant the bomb or break into their home, if drugs were all he really wanted? If he truly hated his wife, why not just divorce her? There were no children to complicate things.

"Emily."

Emily shook out of her thoughts and looked at Kent, his image blurry through her tears. He came close, taking her face gently in his hands. Her tears rolled out and slid down her face. "Emily," he whispered, "this may be a rough night. You may have to spend a night in jail. But I'm doing everything I can to prove you're not involved in this. I need for you to trust God and trust me."

She blinked back her tears and lifted her chin. "I know."

"No, Kent!" Barbara cried. "They can't put her in jail for something she didn't do. You have to stop this!"

Kent let Emily go, turned to Barbara, and looked hard into her eyes. "Calm down, babe. I've got this."

"She's going to jail!" she shouted.

Lance tried to cut in now. "Mom, we'll follow Kent in your car."

"No," she said. "I'm riding with them. You bring the car and meet me there."

"Barbara, it's probably not a good idea for you to ride with us."

"Kent, I'm going with my daughter! Period!" She grabbed a tissue out of the box on the end table and wiped her eyes. "I don't understand why they'd come after her! Are they crazy? Why would she go kill a woman she hardly even knows? She didn't start this! She called the police. She did everything right!"

Emily wanted to tell her mother to calm down, but she focused all her energy on holding herself together. She had been through this before. The humiliating march into the police station, the booking, the search . . .

She lifted her chin higher. She wouldn't die. She had survived this before. She wiped the tears off of her face. "I'm ready to go," she muttered.

Kent walked her out to his car. Emily saw the neighbors standing clustered in their yards. Would they realize she'd been arrested, or would they just think she, Kent, and her mother were going somewhere together? Maybe it looked like a family outing.

An outing where her mother was hysterical and ranting, and police followed behind them.

She supposed she was destined to attract negative attention, no matter how long she was sober. All the hard work, all the right decisions, had done little good. Why had she agreed to move to Atlanta, where her drama had unfolded two years ago? She should have gone someplace new, someplace where they had never heard of her.

She got into the backseat, and her mother climbed in next to her. "Mom, sit up front. The neighbors won't think anything's wrong if you're in the front. I don't want to look like a convict."

Barbara only then seemed to notice the neighbors watching them. She got out and slid into the front as Kent got behind the wheel. Was this how her mother had felt when Emily was arrested before? Always before, she'd been too loaded to care.

"Don't let the police talk to her," Barbara told Kent as he backed out of the driveway. "I'm getting an attorney."

"Barbara, I *am* the police. And Emily has to be the one to ask for the attorney. It's not like it was with Lance. She's not a minor. You won't have any rights here."

"Then you have to protect her, Kent! You're the one who'll be interviewing her."

Kent was quiet for a moment. "Not when they transport her to Birmingham."

Barbara seemed to break down then. Emily saw her mother cover her face, her shoulders shaking. Finally, she spoke again. "Kent, please don't let them keep her. Please. She has to get out tonight."

"I'll do what I can."

Emily closed her eyes and leaned her head back on the seat. Jail. The first time she'd spent a night in jail had been a terrible experience, but this would be even worse, because she hadn't done anything to deserve it.

Her mother drew in a deep, wet breath and took out her phone. "Kent, who should I call? I don't know any attorneys here. Is there someone at church? Someone I could trust?"

He was silent for a moment, and Emily expected him to say that it was a conflict of interest for him to give her the name of an attorney. Instead he said, "She'll need one licensed in Alabama for tomorrow. Call John Stead for tonight, and he can advise her about talking to us. But we've already got

168

her story on record, so I'm not sure he can help."

"I wouldn't have let her talk to you if I'd known she was going to be considered a suspect!" Barbara's voice was filled with contempt and accusation. "I feel tricked."

"Mom, that's not fair," Emily said. "I called *him*."

Emily heard Kent sigh. "You think I tricked her? That I was scheming to implicate Emily?"

"*You* can stop this," Barbara bit out.

"I'm a cop, not a judge," he returned. "I know Emily didn't kill anybody, but the police in Birmingham don't."

Emily felt the dam break, and her tightly held emotions broke free. This was her fault. All her fault. And already she could see the fallout. "I'm sorry I went there, Kent," she said. "You were right. You warned me to leave and come home, but I went ahead and confronted her. Mom, don't blame him. He's helping me."

Silence overtook the car as Kent drove. Emily heard her mother's sobbing breaths in the front seat, saw the muscle in Kent's jaw popping in and out. Could they overcome this, or would her mother keep holding it against him?

Emily closed her eyes and prayed silently

as they drove to the police station. She couldn't lose it now. She had to get a grip. Had to take these panicked thoughts captive.

She racked her mind for something to hang onto, something that had calmed her before.

When I said, "My foot is slipping," your love, oh Lord, supported me. When anxiety was great within me, your consolation brought joy to my soul.

Since getting out of rehab, she'd used that verse like a constant prayer, and God had always proved it true. She breathed it in, held it ballooned in her lungs, then let it flow out — the words of Scripture. More peace washed over her, and strength filtered through her body and mind.

She clung to it as they pulled up to the police station.

CHAPTER 28

Lance followed Kent in his mother's car, a million surreal thoughts racing through his mind. So his sister had problems. She had overcome them. She wasn't a killer.

He tried to think like a cop. Were these cops good at what they did, like most of the police he'd known, or were they inept? How good could they be if they thought Emily was the killer?

His stomach felt sour, and his head was beginning to throb. It had already been a long day.

He thought of April and the plans they'd had tonight. He should call her, let her know what was happening.

He hit a red light and dialed April's number. No answer. Maybe she was in another room of her house, away from her phone. She only lived a few blocks from here. He could swing by, let her know he couldn't go out tonight. Maybe she'd bail on Tyson. He rehearsed what to tell her. This would all be cleared up soon, and Emily would be out. The last thing she needed was talk of another murder adding to the reputation she already had.

If he were Emily, he'd take off to college in North Dakota or somewhere, where nobody had a clue who she was. He supposed even there they might recognize her, since she had been on the national news for a number of days. But it couldn't be as bad as Atlanta, where she went missing and everybody and his dog had been looking for her.

He turned right toward April's house, losing sight of Kent's car. He hoped his mom didn't notice and freak out more.

April's mother came to the door. "Hey, Lance," she said with Georgia sweetness, though she looked like she'd been crying. April had said her mother cried a lot over her marriage problems. "April didn't tell me you were coming."

"She didn't know. I just tried to call her, but she didn't answer."

"I think she was on with someone else," she said.

Great, Lance thought. Probably talking to Tyson.

"Come on in. I'll get her."

He stepped in and fidgeted in the doorway. Finally April came, the phone still to her ear. Covering it with her hand, she whispered, "What are you doing here?"

He didn't want to tell her anything with Tyson on the phone. "I have to tell you something, but I can wait until you get off."

"Okay, just a minute," she whispered. "It's Tyson. Come sit down."

He dropped onto her couch, and she sat next to him, her feet under her. She was so pretty. He hated the way her face lit up when she talked to that guy. Sometimes it lit up that way when she talked to him, too. But maybe he'd waited too long to do anything about it.

"Listen," she said into the phone, "let me call you right back."

Lance breathed relief as she hung up. "Are you okay?" she asked.

"No. Something really bad has happened to my sister, but I can't go into it."

"Is she all right? Is she hurt?"

"No. She just got blamed for something she didn't do." He told her what he knew. "You can't tell a soul. Not your mom, not Tyson, not anybody."

"No, I won't."

"But I can't go tonight. I have to help my mom."

"Okay, of course."

He lingered there. "But I don't want you to go, either."

April seemed amused. "I'm not a little kid, Lance. I can hold my own with Tyson."

He doubted that was true. "I really don't want you to go."

"That's silly. It's no big deal."

He closed his eyes and leaned his head back, looked at the ceiling. "Okay . . . if he's wired, if his pupils are tight . . . or if they're dilated . . . just, anything weird, don't go with him. It's not worth it, okay?"

"Lance, you act like a big brother. I like it."

Fan stinkin' tastic, he thought. The last thing he wanted to be was April's big brother. "I just don't want you to get caught in anything you can't handle. That guy is bad, bad news."

"It'll be fine."

"Anything happens, call me. I'll come get you somehow."

"In what?"

"In my mother's car. How do you think I got here?"

"Okay. I'll call. I hope your sister will be all right."

"Yeah, I'm sure we'll get it all cleared up."
Even as he said it, he knew it wasn't likely.

Cassandra Price would have to wake up from the dead. Or the killer would come out of the shadows and confess like in one of those old detective flicks.

Like that was gonna happen.

She walked him out to the car, stood there watching as he drove away. She was going to go out with Tyson, and Lance couldn't stop it. But too much was out of his control tonight. He sure hoped God was paying attention.

CHAPTER 29

It was a different thing, being arrested and thrown into jail for something she didn't do. But no one at the jail gave Emily the benefit of the doubt. The guards treated her like a criminal.

If she couldn't prove her innocence, she might end up in prison for years. Maybe the rest of her life. Both Georgia and Alabama had a death penalty for murder.

The six-inch pad on the top bunk was a huge step down from her comfortable mattress and comforter at home.

Her cellmate, a thirty-something woman named Hattie, was suffering through withdrawal from painkillers — with fever, nausea, and other flu-like symptoms. Jail was the worst place to detox from a drug like that. In hospitals, they gave you meds to keep you from having seizures, and the nausea and intense flu-like symptoms were more bearable if you knew your caretakers wouldn't let you die. But here, no one cared how lousy you felt.

Hattie retched into the toilet. Emily slid off her bed and touched the woman's back. When she didn't recoil, she bent over and pulled Hattie's dirty hair back from her face. She'd been through this herself, detoxing in a prison of sorts, with no one to help her through it. She didn't know what Hattie had done to get herself put in jail, but it probably had its roots in drug abuse. Most of the people in jail committed crimes for the same reason.

Finally, Hattie stopped retching and sat back on the concrete floor. Emily got a paper towel, wet it, and put it on the back of Hattie's neck. "Are you okay?"

"I think so. For now."

As Hattie sat back on the floor, Emily lowered to the cement facing her, leaning back against the wall next to the toilet. Dark circles hung under Hattie's eyes. "Been there, done that," Emily said. "It gets better, but in the beginning it's no fun."

"I shoulda gone to treatment last time," Hattie said. "Stupid, holding up a convenience store."

Emily winced. "Armed robbery?"

"Yeah." The girl's face was ashen, as if her heart couldn't pump blood all the way to her face. "Man, this ain't me. This ain't how I was raised."

"I know," Emily said.

"No, I mean really. I grew up in church, walkin' the straight and narrow. Used to sing in the choir. Solos, even." Her eyes filled with tears, and she took the paper towel out of Emily's hand and wiped her mouth. "I was really a good singer."

"I understand. I was raised that way, too. I bet you're still a good singer."

The woman looked at the wet paper towel. "And then I was in a car accident, broke my back. Doctors got me started on Oxycontin for the pain. Before I knew it, I was dependent. Needed more and more to fight the pain."

Emily couldn't imagine dealing with severe back pain in a place like this. Hattie was going to have a tough time. "Did you tell your doctor you were getting dependent?"

"He knew. He warned me. And at first I was real careful. But then . . ."

Emily knew the drill. At first the pills deadened the pain — physical and emotional. Then your body built a tolerance, and you needed more to get the same effect. Then came the day when you knew that if you got one more bottle and raised the dose another time, you'd be in total bondage. And your life would be about drugs and nothing else.

And she understood making the decision to go on using.

She fully understood being desperate enough to hold up a convenience store for drug money. "If you can talk to your lawyer, have him ask the judge to send you to treatment. He might. A lot of judges are pro-recovery."

"No, he done that once already. I jumped bond, didn't go to treatment, violated probation. And now here I am. Still gotta live with the pain, but I gotta do it here."

Emily didn't know what to say. Being without hope was even worse than drug detox. She took Hattie's hand. "Can I pray for you?"

The woman's face twisted, and color seeped back into her cheeks. "Yes," she whispered.

Emily scooted closer and put her arms around her, pressed her head against Hattie's, and asked God to help with Hattie's withdrawals, with her physical pain, and with her legal problems. Then she asked him to give her peace. Before she ended the prayer, Hattie interjected her own sorrow at what she'd done, and asked God to forgive her. They both wept as they brought the prayer to an end.

When it was over, Hattie hugged Emily back. "You're a blessing," she told her. "Never thought I'd find a Christian in here. Do you think I could really be a child of God and do the things I done?"

Emily drew in a deep breath. "I guess it doesn't really matter what we were before . . . what matters is what we are now. We're supposed to move forward from wherever we are, and not look back."

"Gon' be hard to do in here."

"I don't know. There are a lot of people here who need him."

"I'd rather they heard about him from somebody else."

Suddenly they were laughing, wiping tears. "Yeah, me too," Emily said. "When I was a little girl, I dreamed of being a ballerina or a rock star. Never thought I'd be sitting in jail. Somehow I don't think this is what God wanted for us."

"Nope. It ain't."

"But he does have a way of using even the bad things. I was scared when I got arrested. Thought I'd be in here with a three-hundred-pound bully who hated blondes."

Hattie laughed again. "Instead you got a hundred-pound loser puking her guts out."

"Hey, that's better than the alternatives. You puke away, girl. We're good."

Later that night, when Hattie's stomach settled, she curled up in pain on her bunk and slept in a fetal position, shivering yet drenched with sweat. Emily gave her her own thin blanket to help with her chills. It was freezing in their cell from the overzealous use of air conditioning, but Emily could take it.

She lay on the top bunk, arms inside her brown jail shirt to keep warm. Outside the cell, she heard the occasional fight break out, profanity flying, and voices echoing over the stone walls in this circle of cells. It was a little taste of hell. Why didn't people take that concept more seriously? Who would want to spend an eternity like this?

Or even another day.

How could she have been so stupid? Why hadn't it even occurred to her that her behavior today looked suspicious?

I was trying to live with integrity, Lord. I was trying to do the Next Right Thing. I promised I would. Why would you let me end up here?

Squeezing her eyes shut, she tried to remember Scripture she'd learned at New Day Treatment Center, where she'd spent a year.

I can do all things through Christ who

181

strengthens me. Did that include suffering for a murder someone else had committed?

Be of sober spirit, be on the alert. Your adversary, the devil, prowls around like a roaring lion, seeking someone to devour.

Man, if that wasn't the truth. Her adversary had done this to her. She had been thoroughly devoured, then spat out to be devoured again.

So either Bo or Carter was to blame for this. Which one would have taken things this far?

She closed her eyes and replayed the afternoon the residents of Haven House had watched the movie. At first, others had been watching, too. Jack, the guy she didn't like because he was constantly stirring up trouble, and Jeffrey, the banker, who sat on the couch fidgeting. Eventually they'd both gotten bored. Analee and Scarlet had watched for the first ten minutes or so, but the need for nicotine and rehab romance had called them back outside.

By the time the conversation took place, only the three of them were left. Carter and Bo, talking about murdering their wives, and Emily behind the desk.

She thought about the character of the two men. By his own admission, Bo was mean when he was intoxicated. He'd confessed to slapping his wife around. He was poor and had several legal challenges. It was possible that things had gone badly when he got home. And if he'd relapsed, he might have had it in him to do the things that had happened today.

But was he smart enough? Emily made it a rule not to give any of them her address or phone number. She knew better than to get too close to anyone at Haven House. Would Bo be smart enough to track her down, make a homemade bomb, and put it under her car? Would he know how to pick a lock? Would he leave the kind of cryptic message he'd left?

Maybe, but Bo seemed more like the kind of person who sat around talking about doing such things, but would never take the initiative to do them.

Carter, on the other hand, had a sly edge. He was a welder, made a little more money, and had a quicker wit. Though he wasn't that savvy on the computer, and rarely joined them on Facebook, he probably could have figured out how to track Emily down. Though she kept a professional distance between them, he did seem to have a bit of a crush on her. She hadn't encouraged it. Maybe that was it. Maybe he felt she'd been too dismissive of him. But it was more than that. If Carter really meant to kill Bo's wife and have Bo return the favor, it was no wonder he'd try to kill the one person who knew the truth.

And when that failed and he was sure that Emily had called the police, he had to figure out a way to discredit her. Pinning the murder of his own wife on Emily with a stolen necklace . . . and the bottle of pills . . . Making Emily look like an active addict had hammered the nail in her coffin. Even her mother and Kent probably had doubts about her now.

She hated herself for not listening to her mother about taking the job at the rehab. But she'd been so careful. There were some residents at Haven House who rode her because she took her job seriously and didn't tolerate people who tried to smuggle drugs in. When someone violated the rules, she reported them for the sake of those who really wanted to change. But some of those she'd gotten thrown out — especially if that meant they had to go to jail — might hold long grudges. But she couldn't think of anything she'd done to make Carter or Bo mad. Nothing for which they'd plan so carefully to ruin her life.

She prayed God would clear her name soon. He was the champion of truth, after all, wasn't he? She wished that knowledge would calm her spirit, help her to sleep in peace. But fear kept her awake, and the threat of tomorrow made her shiver.

CHAPTER 30

Emily's problems had Kent tied in knots.
Part of him wanted to work 24/7 to find the
killer so Emily would go free. But his professional side recognized he had a conflict of
interest. If Emily was a suspect in the Cassandra Price killing, then she had to be
considered a person of interest in the Devon
Lawrence murder. But there was no way,
given his relationship with the family, that
he could interrogate her like a murder
suspect. So he had to make a hard choice.

He sat in his boss's office with Andy and
filled Greg, the chief detective, in on everything he knew. "I think it's best if I remove
myself from this case," he said. "Emily's like
my own daughter. Her mother and I are
close."

"Real close," Andy added. "Like, he-has-
a-ring-in-his-pocket close."

Kent shot him an unappreciative look.

"Really?" Greg said. "You gonna propose,

Harlan?"

"When the time is right. But everything's up in the air right now."

Greg tapped his pencil on his desk in a steady drumbeat. "I can see that. I guess you're right. We can put Strand on the case. Andy can still work it and fill him in."

"Strand?" Kent didn't like that. Strand was a good guy, but he was a brand-new detective, with little experience in homicide. It would take someone with more experience to get the right person behind bars. "Can't you give it to someone with a few more years under his belt?"

"Hey, Andy's experienced. He knows everything you know about the case. It'll be fine."

"It's just that . . . Emily's a good kid. Two years sober. Good student. She didn't do this."

"And your bias is exactly why you're turning over the case. You've done the right thing. Now let them work it. You'll work with Joe while this is going on."

Joe, Strand's partner, was a good detective, but he had a chip on his shoulder. Kent didn't look forward to it. "I'm just saying, I don't want anybody stopping short of finding the real killer, just because they have somebody to nail it on."

Greg looked offended. "Are you suggesting anybody on my team would do that?"

"No, of course not."

"Do *you* do that?"

"No, never. But psychologically, if you're not experienced, you tend to jump to conclusions, and the power of suggestion can lead you down the wrong track. Strand may not have the instincts he needs to sort out truth from lies."

Andy grunted. " 'Preciate the vote of confidence, partner. Listen — you have to trust me. And brace yourself for the results of this case, even if you don't like them."

Kent left the office feeling sick. Maybe he'd done the wrong thing. Now he had no control.

It was ten o'clock when he went home, where Barbara and Lance were trying to get settled into his house. He found Barbara in the back, changing the sheets on his bed. He liked the way she looked moving among his things. She hadn't yet noticed him, and he watched her for a moment before saying her name.

When she looked up, her eyes were swollen, bare of makeup, and the frown lines between her eyes seemed more deeply etched. He knew she wouldn't take his bowing out very well. It had taken hours for her to finally accept that Emily wasn't coming home tonight and leave the police station. She wouldn't sleep tonight.

"This house sure is brighter with you in it," he said.

The comment did nothing to take that look of devastation from her face. "Kent, do they still have to transport her to Birmingham tomorrow?"

He sighed. "Yes. There was nothing I could do about that. A state patrol officer will come to get her."

She turned away, tucked a corner of the sheet in. "Can I ride with her?"

"No, babe. I'm sorry."

"Can *you* ride with her? Or transport her yourself?"

"No." He stepped up behind her, took her shoulders.

"I had to take myself off the case because of the conflict of interest."

She swung around and gaped at him. "You did *what?*"

"I had to, Barbara."

"But why? You may have been the only one thinking clearly! You know all the details . . . how she called you and called the Birmingham police, how she told everything she knew as soon as she figured it out . . ."

"Andy and Strand know that, too."

"Strand? The new guy? Are you kidding me? You said he's green, that he doesn't have the instincts."

He never should have told her that about a colleague. "He'll be okay. *She'll* be okay."

She couldn't even look at him, just turned away and finished making the bed.

"Barbara? Are you mad at me?"

"Yes!" She spun back around. "I was depending on you to get her off. I thought you would work tirelessly to find the killer. That you wouldn't let this stand."

"I still won't."

"But now she's at the mercy of Andy and some guy who barely passed the detective exam!"

"I know this is hard, Barbara. But I'm sworn to uphold the law, and when there's a conflict of interest, I'm duty-bound to give it to someone else. And the last thing Emily needs is some prosecutor claiming she got special treatment and consideration because her mother's boyfriend was investigating the case."

"So you're going to be totally uninvolved?"

"No, I'll stay on top of things. I'll still be informed."

"But they won't listen to you now! When you tell them Emily is innocent, they won't believe you!"

"Barbara, trust me. Trust God. Emily's innocent. I know that. But with that kind of bias, I couldn't do a thorough investigation of her as a person of interest."

She lowered herself to the edge of the bed, staring into the air at some unseen horror. "They're going to treat her like a murderer. All the stuff they said about her two years ago is going to come rushing back into this case, and her two years of hard work on sobriety, and her good grades, and the changes in her life are going to go up in smoke!"

"We won't let it. We'll fight this together. I'm not dropping out of her life. Just off the case. I'm still there for her, and for you."

"But you're there as another person who has no control. What good is that?"

She pushed past him into the small kitchen, where Lance sat staring at a textbook. Kent followed her, but he didn't know what else to say. She could barely look at him, much less speak to him.

He felt the ring in his pocket and wondered if he'd ever be able to give it to her now. The possibility that her answer would be no burned in his chest. He'd been presumptuous buying it when he did. He should have waited.

When it was clear she had nothing more to say to him, he said, "Guess I'll go now."

Lance looked up. "Where?"

"To your house. I'll spend the night there. You two make yourselves at home. There's a little food in the fridge. Clean towels, I think."

"Why are you even going over there if you're not on the case anymore?" Barbara asked him coldly.

"Because I'm still a cop, and I still want to catch this guy. If he comes back, I'll be there."

"No," Barbara said. "You stay here, and we'll go to a hotel."

"Barbara, this is not negotiable," Kent said more firmly. "I'm not on the case, but I care about this family. I'm staying at your house, and there's no more discussion."

He tried not to slam the door on his way out.

CHAPTER 31

Emily's ride to Birmingham the next morning in a state trooper's car was quiet. Her driver wasn't interested in chatting with a murder suspect. She sat in the backseat of the patrol car, watching out the window as she rode, wondering if her mother would come to Birmingham, if she'd found her an attorney there, if she had any shot at getting out on bond. And what was Dr. Ingles thinking about her test? Did he think she'd just blown it off, or had he seen something about her arrest on the news? At least there hadn't been any press waiting when she was picked up this morning. Maybe the Atlanta media hadn't yet gotten word.

Even if the Birmingham judge set bond, how would her mother pay it? She was just digging out from her debts from Emily's dark days. Would this set them back again? Or would those pills on the counter convince her mom Emily was using? Would that tough love muscle kick in? Would her mother fight for Emily's freedom if she had such doubts?

When they got to the jail in Birmingham, Emily braced herself for rough treatment. Her shackles rattled as she walked into the building — heralding the fact that she was accused of a violent crime — and went through the normal booking routine.

A woman with wild, white hair and wilder eyes was being booked, and at the sight of Emily, she began wailing. "She da one!" the woman cried. "She strangled my mama!"

"What?" Emily said.

"Don't worry about it," the booking officer muttered in her ear. "Cass's been here a dozen times. Her mother's not even dead."

Emily just looked at the woman whose face was twisted in misery. Why did they have her in jail, when she belonged in a mental hospital?

They took Emily's mug shots, and on the way out, as they stepped down the stairs, Cass stepped on Emily's shackles. Emily fell and caught herself on the railing, and the guard reached out to right her. Pain shot through her ankle.

"Step back, Cass!" the guard shouted. Two other guards came running and restrained the crazy woman.

"You okay?" one of the guards asked Emily grudgingly.

"I twisted my ankle, but I'm okay." She got up, keeping her weight on her good foot. It wouldn't be good to show weakness in a place like this. Slowly, she put weight back on her left foot, and pain ripped through her.

Sweat broke out on her face as she limped the rest of the way down to the basement. They took her to a small room and uncuffed her hands, though they left her feet shackled. "Sit down," the guard said. "The detectives want to question you."

She wondered if it was the same detective she'd spoken to yesterday. She would probably try to trip her up and find inconsistencies in her story. She leaned on the table and prayed that God would help her to be convincing. The truth was her only weapon. If they didn't believe it . . . what else did she have?

After a few minutes, a man stepped into the room. He looked a little like Matt Damon, and he was young — around thirty — and smiled as though they were friends. "Emily, I'm Noel Gosling. Your mother hired me this morning."

An attorney! Relief and gratitude flooded through her. She was suddenly self-conscious about how she looked. Her face bare of makeup, her hair stringy and un- washed, brown prison clothes — and brown wasn't her best color. Quickly, she snatched her thoughts back. How could she be wor- ried about her looks when she was sitting here charged with murder?

She shook his hand. "Is my mother here?"

"On her way. We talked by phone."

"Boy, am I glad to see you. I really ap- preciate your coming." She leaned toward him as he took a seat. "I'm innocent. You've got to get me out of this. We've got to get this cleared up before it gets any worse. And my family could be in danger. I'm worried about them."

"I have a feeling the person setting you up for this'll back off if you're in jail. He wants them to believe you're doing all this."

Thank you, God! He believed in her in- nocence. "Then my mom told you the story?"

Noel nodded and opened a legal pad. "Yep. It sounds just crazy enough to be true. I also talked to John Stead in Atlanta. He's a good friend of mine."

John was an attorney Emily knew from church, who worked with college-aged kids — probably the one who'd given her mother this referral.

"He vouched for your character and integrity since you've been in Atlanta. I trust his judgment."

"It's those years before rehab that make me look bad."

"People change. I think your story is inspiring."

She liked him and began to relax. "Look, I know you're going to tell me not to talk to the police, but I want to. I want to tell them whatever they want to know, make them understand."

"That's why I'm here." His speech was crisp, with just a touch of southern drawl. "They'll come in to interview you in a few minutes. I'll be present, and if I touch your arm or interrupt you, I want you to stop talking."

"I have nothing to hide."

"Still, don't tell them anything unless they ask you. The more you volunteer, the more you might get tripped up. They can read things into your statement that you don't want read into it."

"But the truth is the truth!" she said. "I won't get tripped up if I tell the truth."

"Trust me, Emily. Just answer their questions. No speculation, no extra information. Now, I want you to go over everything with me before they come in. Start to finish. Take

197

your time. They're not coming until we're finished."

Emily drew in a deep breath and told him the story. When she was finished, she studied the attorney's face. Yes, he seemed to believe her. She watched as he made notes in a small binder. "Noel, is there any chance they'll set bond so I can get out of here today?"

"We'll push for it, but if I know this judge, he might not. Especially if he has to let you go back to Atlanta."

"But there's a possibility?"

"If we see the judge today, I'll do everything in my power. Meanwhile, do you want water or anything?"

"That'd be nice. But could you ask them to take the shackles off? I twisted my ankle on the way down the stairs."

Noel looked down at her foot, rolled up her pant leg, and gasped at the swelling. "Emily, why didn't you tell me this up front?"

"It's not the most important thing going on, but it really hurts."

"I'll get these taken off right away."

Noel went out and talked to the police, and in moments they came in and released the shackles and brought her a bag of ice. She propped her foot on another folding chair and tried not to think about the pain.

When the two cops came in — a woman and a man — Emily prayed silently that God would open their hearts and make them believe her. They introduced themselves as Detective Stone — whom she'd spoken to yesterday — and Detective Piper. She dropped her foot and rose slightly as she shook their hands, said yes ma'am and yes sir, and hoped they'd make note of the fact that she was respectful.

"So, Emily," Detective Stone said in a voice kinder than she'd used on the phone, "you know that you're here because we issued a warrant for your arrest in connection with Cassandra Price's death."

"Yes."

Stone sipped her coffee. "Where were you when you made that call to me yesterday?"

"I was at school in Atlanta," she said. "But I came to Birmingham after that to warn Cassandra, because I didn't think you were taking me seriously."

Noel touched her hand, probably warning her not to put the detectives on the defensive.

Detective Piper spoke up. "She reported that you were following her yesterday afternoon." His voice was gruffer, louder, no-nonsense.

"I was. I wanted to tell her the whole story, but I guess I spooked her when I left her a message earlier. She wouldn't talk to me. She accused me of having a thing for her husband." She glanced at Noel, felt her cheeks warming. "That wasn't true. Not at all. I only knew him from working at Haven House and haven't communicated with him since he got out. He was married and way too old for me —"

Noel squeezed her arm again.

"I talked to Kent Harlan at the Atlanta PD, and he told me to come home, not to do anything else in Birmingham. So I did."

They went over her timeline, moment by moment. Emily knew her phone records would verify everything. They had her repeat her account of the *Strangers on a Train* incident at Haven House. Finally, after what seemed like hours of grilling, Noel spoke up. "My client has accounted for her time at length. You have the report of the time she approached Cassandra and the time that Emily's mother reported their home break-in. Detective Kent Harlan has verified when she returned to Atlanta."

Emily nodded. "And weren't there police who talked to Cassandra after she reported me following her?"

"Yes," Stone said. "I spoke to her."

"Then they can confirm that she was alive *after* I left Birmingham. I didn't see her again. I went straight home. There's no way I could have gotten home when I did if I'd stayed long enough to kill her."

The male detective scowled and seemed to study his notes. "Emily, do you own a necklace with your initials on them?" he asked.

Emily closed her eyes. "Yes, but it must have been stolen from my house yesterday. I haven't even worn it in a couple of weeks."

"It was found near the body of Cassandra Price."

"I know. They asked me about it in Atlanta. But that's all part of the setup."

The detectives looked unconvinced.

"Don't you see? It was even part of the movie. There was a lighter with the lead guy's initial on it, and the bad guy carries it around the whole movie. Bo or Carter — whichever it is — is trying to set me up for this murder. They're trying to pin all this on me, and they've planned it right down to the necklace with my initials. Check them out — find out where they were at the time of the killings and the break-in. One of them did this!"

"According to the Atlanta PD," Stone said, "Bo was at work at the time of his

201

wife's murder, and his whereabouts at the time of Cassandra's have been established as well. Carter Price was at work at the time of *his* wife's murder. Dozens of people have confirmed that he was there. You're the only one who can't account for all of your time in Birmingham."

Emily's heart sank. That couldn't be. They couldn't *both* have ironclad alibis. "No way! Did you ask Carter about the movie, and the conversation they had?"

"Yes, we did. He claims it was all a joke."

"But it wasn't, because now both those women are dead!" She slammed her hand on the table with the last word. "I told you this was going to happen. If I were the murderer, why would I do that? Why would I connect these two murders that wouldn't have been connected? Does that even make sense to you?" Sweat broke out on her temples.

"Tell us about your drug abuse, Emily."

Here we go. She leaned back. "I've been clean for two years."

"None of that has anything to do with this case," Noel interjected.

"They tested me when I was booked, so you know I'm clean," Emily said. "I've been working hard and minding my own business until somebody duct-taped a bomb under my car."

The male cop made a couple of notes, then looked up at Emily. "How many times did you meet Cassandra Price?"

"When Carter was in rehab, twice maybe? They only got visiting days one Saturday a month. I hardly exchanged two words with her either time."

"How close did you get to Carter?"

"Not close at all. I just knew him."

"Did he talk about his marriage?"

"Yes. That day he said he hated his wife. Blamed her for his getting arrested and sent to rehab. Bo did, too."

"Was there ever any flirtation between you?"

"Detectives," Noel cut in, "my client doesn't have to —"

"Wait!" Emily said, leaning on the table. "I have to answer this. They did flirt. A lot of the guys at the rehab did. But I didn't flirt back. I know they're vulnerable when they're in treatment, and the truth is, I think it's a bad idea to mix men and women in rehab. They focus on each other instead of on recovery, and there are devastating affairs . . . even the married clients. When I was in treatment, all the clients were women. At Haven House, I keep a professional distance. The last thing I want in my life is another addict. I wasn't even buddy-buddy watching the movie with them. I was behind my desk in the same room the whole time."

"Did you play a part in that *Strangers on a Train* scheme, Emily? Maybe plan to make the murders go three ways?"

"Absolutely not! Like I said, why would I call your attention to it if I was implicating *myself?*"

"Maybe to throw us off when the murders actually happened?"

"So you think I bombed my own car and broke into my own house and wrote on my own wall?"

They didn't answer, but she knew they were thinking that suspects did things to throw them off all the time.

This wasn't going well. She felt like Joseph from the Bible, thrown into a jail cell for something she hadn't done. But she wasn't as stoic as the famous Joseph, and there wasn't a pharaoh whose dreams she could interpret.

No good could come from this.

CHAPTER 32

As discouragement sank its talons into her, Emily wished she had died of an overdose back in her drug days. Her mom never would have had her memories stained by the trauma that had poisoned their lives for the past several years, or the fallout that continued long after she'd vowed to stay sober.

She wasn't going to see the judge today, so she would have to stay in jail at least one more night. And if the judge didn't set bond, she would stay indefinitely.

The sounds of steel doors sliding shut vibrated through Emily's head, her back, her swollen foot. Murder. When she got up yesterday morning, she never would have believed it.

How had a simple movie prompted such an evil sequence of events?

She sat down at the steel table in her cell. Her new Birmingham cellmate — who mercifully was not the crazy woman who tripped her — was out on the work crew. On the desk was a stack of paper and envelopes that the county had given her. She had a pen without a case, just the bendable cartridge and the metal tip. Did they think they'd stab each other with the plastic casing?

She thought of Cass and realized that was a possibility. She was thankful they'd put the woman in lockdown. She should be thankful for the precautions, even on the pens.

Two shrieking, catty voices rose over the noise outside her cell, and profanity flew as something crashed. An alarm sounded and doors clanged open. Guards came running in to break up the fight.

She went to the open doorway and stared out at the common area where the inmates congregated. The guards were forcing two women to the ground, dragging them across the floor. She supposed they'd be taken to lockdown, too. Maybe things would be quiet for a while.

The bond for murder was always high. Her mom would never be able to post it. Even the percentage required — ten, fifteen percent? — would be way more than they could afford.

All this would further damage her reputation, even after they found the real killer. Once word got out that she'd been arrested for killing Cassandra Price, and she was declared a person of interest in Devon Lawrence's murder, her mother's job would be toast. The architects would have to cut her loose to keep their clients from walking.

But the damage may have already been done. Guilt-by-association would taint her entire family, no matter how innocent they were.

These thoughts weren't getting her anywhere. She had to take them captive. Her cellmate's paperback Bible sat on the desk, and she opened it and thumbed through to Genesis 37, where Joseph's cruel brothers had thrown him into a pit because they were jealous of him. They had sold him like a piece of property, forcing him into a life of slavery.

She'd studied Joseph's story in rehab and had taken copious notes about what she'd learned. It had never occurred to her then that she would need it now. But the similarities stunned her.

Joseph had been wrongfully punished, too. But as a slave, Joseph worked hard and was trustworthy, and ultimately was put in charge of his master's affairs. He didn't

207

whine about his state or the fact that he'd been unfairly sold into bondage.

Then he, like Emily, was falsely accused and thrown into prison. Had he felt like Emily did now, sitting in a cell and wondering how it had come to this? Had he pled with God for rescue? Had he plotted his escape?

The Bible didn't say. All it said was that he rolled up his sleeves and got to work, and every job he was given he did to the best of his ability, until finally, he was put in charge of all the inmates. He was a man of integrity, and that integrity guided him even in the darkest places. He worked for the Lord, not for men, so he did his best no matter what he was given to do. He'd stayed in prison for years — all for something he hadn't done.

Emily closed her eyes and rubbed her temples, then got up and went back to the door to her cell, and gazed out on all the prisoners in the common area, some tough and dangerous, others quiet and grief-stricken, playing cards or reading or doing push-ups or trash-talking. What if God made her suffer through this?

She wondered if Joseph ever felt abandoned by God. How had he managed to trust his creator so?

The story, better than any novel, had climaxed when famine hit, and his brothers came to Egypt to buy food. Instead of hatred and revenge, he gave them gifts and forgave them. "What you intended for evil," he said, "God intended for good."

Emily closed the Bible and tried once again to imagine what good could come from her own story. No matter how hard she tried, she couldn't see it. Lives would be devastated if she had to stay here. Her mom and Lance would be humiliated and crushed. Her Christian witness, which she'd worked hard on during these months of sobriety, would be tainted.

Maybe she just didn't have the kind of integrity that Joseph had. After all, she had succumbed to the lure of drug addiction. On her worst day, she was really no better than Bo or Carter. She had lied and stolen and cheated to keep her drugging lifestyle going. No, she'd never killed anyone. But she probably deserved much more jail time than she'd gotten.

The realization made her feel hopeless. She stretched out on her rack and laid her wrist over her eyes. God knew of failure. He had watched David, who really had killed a man after getting the guy's wife pregnant . . . Peter, who'd betrayed Jesus three times . . .

Paul, who'd murdered Christians . . . Mary Magdalene, who'd been a wild child.

Yet they had all been exalted people of faith, talked about for centuries. If they could do it, Emily could. She could still do this, even if God didn't clear her. And if he didn't, there would be a reason. A purpose that she would let him fulfill.

She squeezed her eyes shut and pressed her palms against her eyes. "God, whatever happens, please don't leave me. I want to be someone you're proud of. Someone who doesn't humiliate my family. I trust you with whatever you're about to do."

But the ceiling seemed stone cold. She only hoped her prayers took wing.

Chapter 33

Barbara had seen Emily in prison clothes before, but defeat assaulted her as her daughter was brought into the courtroom with her hands chained together in front of her. Barbara caught her breath when she saw that she was limping, her left foot swollen inside the orange prison-issue flip-flop. When she met Emily's eyes, she saw dark circles and fear.

In the brown prison clothes and chains, her hair stringy, Emily looked like any of the guilty defendants paraded through here for the judge to see. He wouldn't know that Emily wasn't like them — that she was a college journalism major with a future.

Kent sat next to Barbara, his foot tapping a nervous, quiet drumbeat. Tension still hung between them, though she hadn't been able to stay mad at him when he offered to drive her to Birmingham. He was only trying to do the right thing by taking himself off the case. She didn't like it, but she couldn't blame him anymore. He was a man of integrity, and that was why she loved him.

They sat through the other capital murder and violent crime cases — a man accused of causing brain damage to his three-month-old baby after shaking him, a woman who'd murdered her cousin over a man, a gang member who'd gunned down an enemy. How could they lump Emily together with these thugs?

Finally, it was Emily's turn before the judge. The lawyer Barbara had hired met Emily at the bench. Emily limped to the podium where she was supposed to speak into a microphone. She stood with shoulders slumped. From the back, she looked broken.

As Emily entered her plea — not guilty — and the attorney requested that she be released on bond, Barbara burst into tears. Barbara couldn't hold it together. She shaded her eyes and looked down as tears assaulted her again. She fantasized about springing up and screaming out that Emily was innocent. But the last thing she wanted was to make Emily's situation worse.

Kent reached into his sport coat, pulled out a handkerchief, and handed it to her. She took it gratefully and wiped her nose, her eyes.

"I'll set bond at five hundred thousand dollars, pending indictment," the judge said. "Emily, you can return to Atlanta, but you're not authorized to travel more than one hundred fifty miles from Birmingham, and if you're indicted and fail to appear, you'll forfeit the bond money and be incarcerated without bond."

Barbara touched Kent's arm. Was the judge really going to let her come home . . . for half a million dollars?

As Emily turned to leave, she turned back toward Barbara, her mouth twisted and her forehead pleated. She appeared on the verge of tears as she limped toward the door. Her eyes seemed to ask, *Five hundred thousand? What are we gonna do?*

Court adjourned, and as the others in the pew-like seats got up to leave, Barbara sat frozen, unable to move. Kent took her hand. "It's okay, babe. Ten percent of that is all we have to come up with."

"Fifty thousand dollars? I don't have that! Where am I gonna get it?"

The guard asked them to clear the room, so Barbara got to her feet. She straightened her skirt and jacket and forced herself to move. She felt Kent's hand on her elbow, steadying her as she went out to her car.

"I'll help with this," he said before they got in. "I have equity in my house. I can get a credit line."

She thought about that for a moment. Yes, a credit line. That was a possibility. "I have equity, too. At least that much. I can get a second mortgage."

"I don't want you doing that," Kent said. "Just let me."

She grunted and gaped at him. "Why would I let *you* do that?"

Her question seemed to hurt him. He swallowed and slipped his hand into his pocket. "Because you're family to me. I love you. I love Emily, too. I want to do it."

Her eyes filled with tears, and she stepped closer to him. "I can't let you do that, Kent."

"Why not? She's innocent. We'll get it all back once she goes back to court . . . one way or another."

One way or another? She lost it then, right there.

He put his arms around her and pulled her close. She shut her eyes and rested her chin on his shoulder. Though her burden seemed crushing, it felt as though he was helping her lift it. She wasn't in this alone. "It'll be okay," he whispered.

She wept into his shirt, comforted by his arms. But she couldn't let herself fall apart

214

like this. She had to be strong. If she was going to get Emily out today, they had to hurry back to Atlanta and figure something out.

She drew in a long, cleansing breath and forced herself to straighten. "I can't stand here crying. Emily's stuck in there until I come up with the cash. Let's go."

They got into the car, and Kent pulled out of the parking lot into the traffic streaming by.

"I'll go to the bank and try to get it," she said. "If I can't, you can help. But only then."

"I wish you'd let me do more." They got to a red light, and he took her hand. It was rough, strong, rock solid.

She brought his hand to her face, kissed the knuckle. "I love you for wanting to. But I need a lot more from you than money. Solve this crime, on-duty or off. Stop the person doing this. Don't let them destroy Emily."

Kent knew better than to make that promise.

CHAPTER 34

Back in Atlanta, Barbara asked Kent to go into her house with her while she gathered all the papers the bank might require. He went back to work while she went to the bank.

At her branch, each loan officer was already helping another customer, so she waited on an uncomfortable couch and fidgeted until one of the loan officers came out.

The woman who would decide Emily's fate had a beehive hairdo and unfriendly eyes, though she offered a business smile. "Were you next?"

"Yes." Barbara sprang to her feet, dropping the papers that were on her lap. Feeling like an idiot, she stooped down and scooped them up — the appraisal for her house, the financial statements, her tax returns. She stacked the pages haphazardly, followed the woman back in, and took one of the chairs facing the desk. She noticed a newspaper sitting on the credenza. Had Emily been mentioned in the paper? She hadn't taken the time to look yet.

There was no way the local reporters would keep an item like that off the front page — if it wasn't there today, it would be tomorrow.

She drew in a deep breath. "Uh . . . I was thinking about maybe getting a line of credit on the equity in my house. The appraisal is fairly recent. I just bought the house a few months ago."

Ms. Green took the appraisal, scanned it. "And how much do you owe on the house?"

"I have the mortgage papers right here." Barbara slid them across the desk. "I sold my house in Missouri, so I was able to put two hundred thousand dollars down when I bought this house."

"Okay. The market probably hasn't changed much. The appraisal is still good, and you're not getting all of the equity out."

"Oh, good." Barbara tried to steady her breath.

The woman pulled out a loan application. "What do you need the money for?"

She hesitated too long, trying to arrange her words. *To bond my daughter out of jail* wouldn't cut it. "I need to pay off some debts."

"How much do you want?"

"Just sixty thousand. That's . . . enough for now." That would pay for the bond and cover the retainer for the attorney . . . if Emily wasn't indicted. If she was, Barbara would need a lot more.

The woman went through the other papers she'd brought, asking her a few more questions. Then she walked her through an application for a home equity credit line.

"I'll just run this by the mortgage division, but I should be able to give you an answer this afternoon."

Barbara tried not to look too anxious. "Okay. The sooner the better. I . . . have some bills due right now, and . . . it would be good if I could pay them off. When would I be able to get a check?"

"If we approve it this afternoon, you could get the money before we close today."

"Oh, good. Great. That'll help a lot."

She waited as Ms. Green went to make copies of all her papers. As she waited, she sat stiffly in the chair, her eyes closed.

God, if they don't approve it today, they'll see the paper and hear the gossip. They won't approve it tomorrow. Please . . . I need your help. Don't make Emily stay in jail.

218

Ms. Green came back and handed Barbara the papers. "I'll call you this afternoon," she said. Barbara shook her hand, hoping the woman didn't notice that her palms were sweating. Then she stepped out into the warm air.

She went back to Kent's and waited, phone in hand. The banker didn't call until 4:30. She'd been approved for the loan, and the papers were ready to sign. She raced back to the bank and tried not to look frantic as she signed the papers. Then she went to the teller's window and asked for a money order for fifty thousand dollars out of her credit line.

She hoped the bondsman would accept that. She knew from her last experience with a bondsman that they rarely took checks.

She headed back to Birmingham, praying that they'd let her bond Emily out even though it was after business hours. She got a bondsman on the phone, and after giving Barbara the third degree about Emily and her charges, he agreed to meet her at the jail. It would cost more because Emily was leaving the state, he told her, but he would take a personal check for the difference to bond her out.

Barbara felt numb as she found the jail and went in, talked with the bondsman in the stairwell, and arranged the deal as if it were somehow under the table. But that was how it was done. The money was collateral to assure that Emily would show up in court, and the bondsman charged a pretty penny for it.

When the deal was done, he directed her to the dirty waiting room at the jail. After he went over the terms of the agreement with Emily, she would be released, he said. As Barbara waited, her mind raced with thoughts about their next move. At least Emily wouldn't have to spend another night in jail, and they would be safe at Kent's house.

Emily discarded her jail clothes and dressed in the clothes she'd been arrested and transported in, but she couldn't get her left shoe on. She held the shoe in her hand as she met with the bondsman.

When her paperwork was processed and she was free to go, Emily limped through the door into the waiting area. Her mother rose to her feet, and Emily studied her face, trying to anticipate her mood. Whatever she'd had to do to raise fifty thousand dollars had probably dredged up dark memories. But instead of hurling accusations, her mom came to her with arms outstretched and hugged her fiercely. As she clung to Emily, stroking her hair, she whispered, "Are you okay?"

"Yes, I'm fine." Emily blinked back tears. "I thought I would have to stay here when I heard the amount."

"I got the money," her mom said. "We're going to clear your name, and everything will be all right. What happened to your foot?"

"Twisted it."

"Did somebody hurt you?"

She shrugged as if it were no big deal. "I got crossways with a crazy woman who thought I'd strangled her mother."

"Emily! She hit you?"

"No, she just pushed me. My ankle twisted on the stairs." She limped to the car, anxious to get far away from the jail.

Barbara unlocked the car on the passenger side, and Emily got in. "Let me see."

Emily pulled her foot up. It was swollen like a football, and had bruised purple.

"That's wrong," Barbara blurted. "They should protect the inmates."

"She's in lockdown now. Let's just get out of here."

Her mother was speechless as they pulled out of the parking lot. Emily hoped she never had to see this place again.

CHAPTER 35

We're going out again 2night. Wanna come?

Lance frowned down at April's text. He typed back, *Who is we?*

Tyson & me. He's fun 2 hang out with.

Lance groaned. "Unbelievable," he said aloud.

Emily sat sideways on Kent's couch, where she'd sat since getting home from jail tonight, her foot encased in an ice pack and propped on a pillow. "What's wrong?"

"April," Lance said. "She's getting too friendly with this dude named Tyson. He's bad news."

"I thought you had a thing for April."

"I do," he admitted. "I just haven't told her yet. I don't want to ruin our friendship."

"Well, you'd better make your move."

Lance knew she was right. April had been evasive about her time with Tyson. "She wants me to hang out with them tonight. I feel like a third wheel, but I don't trust him with her."

"She wouldn't have invited you if she wanted to be alone with him," Emily said. "That's a good sign."

"You think?"

"Yeah. You should go."

Emily looked so pale and fragile that Lance didn't want to leave her. "But you just got home."

"I'm fine," she said. "Just glad to be here. Go and protect your territory. It's been a rough couple of days for you, too."

His mother heard from the kitchen. "She's right. Go ahead and go."

They wouldn't feel that way if Lance told them Tyson was a doper who probably sold drugs, and that Lance felt the compulsion to protect April from him. But that was something he'd rather they didn't know. "All right," he said. "Guess I will."

"Where are you guys going?" his mom called.

He shrugged. "Not sure yet. Just hanging out, I guess. Maybe at April's. I'll get them to pick me up."

"Okay, just be home by ten. It's a school night."

Nothing more was said about it, but Lance had a sinking feeling as he showered and got ready. What did April see in Tyson?

Was it the bad-boy image that she liked? Was Lance too predictable? Was he best-friend material, but not boyfriend material?

He knew it was lame going along like this, but he didn't give a flip what Tyson thought. He was going to protect April. That was all that mattered.

He texted Kent's address to April, and told her to have Tyson pick him up there. A little after eight, Tyson's car rumbled up to the curb, and Lance loped out. April was already there, riding shotgun. Lance got into the backseat. "Hey," he said. "Thanks for picking me up."

"No problem, dude." Tyson's hair was greasy and stringy, his face unshaven. He had the stubble of a middle-aged man rather than a high-schooler, and his eyes were bloodshot, as if he hadn't slept in days.

"Why are you here? Whose house is this?" April asked.

"My mom's boyfriend. We were just over here having supper." He didn't want to mention their fear of staying in their own home.

"Everything okay?" she asked him over the seat.

He nodded quietly.

Tyson cranked the music up, a rap song with a vibrating bass line. Lance wanted to tell him to turn it down, but the idiot probably couldn't hear him. The car smelled terrible — some combination of urine, body odor, and smoke. The cushions were split and foam rubber stuffing pebbled out.

Tyson flew way too fast, tapping his hand to the beat. "Where are we going?" Lance finally yelled over the music.

"A special place," Tyson yelled. "I'm taking you to the stars tonight."

"What stars?" April asked, her eyes glistening.

Tyson grinned. "You'll see. Hope you're not afraid of heights."

Her amusement faded. "I am, actually. What is it? The top of a building or something?"

He laughed and ramped the music up higher. "You'll see."

They were on Howard Avenue, almost to the MARTA station. Lance tried to anticipate where they were going.

Tyson suddenly turned the music down. "Ready to learn how to have a good time?" he asked, laughing.

That didn't sound good. Lance braced himself.

Tyson slowed as he reached the train station, got into the right lane, and turned onto Paden, just past the Decatur water tower.

He braked suddenly, then cut a hard right, bouncing over the curb and onto the grass just outside the fence surrounding the tower.

"What are you doing?" April asked, clutching the dashboard.

Tyson grinned and shifted into park. He leaned forward, gazing through the windshield through the darkness to the top of the tower. "You should see things from up there. It's like ten stories up. You go up that little ladder, and you can walk around that catwalk up on the tank. You'll love it."

April looked back at Lance, alarm in her eyes. "No way. I'm not going up there."

"Come on, baby. I want you to see it."

"She's not your baby," Lance clipped. April shot him a surprised look. "We're not going up there," he said. "End of discussion."

Tyson hit the steering wheel and threw up his hands. "Hey, man, you are really tense. You're wound up as tight as a church lady."

Lance thought of walking home. Who did this guy think he was?

"You need a little something to calm your nerves." Tyson reached under his seat, pulled out a cigarette. He got his lighter and clicked on a flame, let it linger on the tip as he put it to his lips and inhaled. As the smoke filled the car, Lance realized it was a joint. "Here, baby," Tyson told April. "Smoke some of this, you'll be so mellow you won't even think about your fear of heights."

"I don't want to do that," April said in a low voice.

"Why not? We did it last night."

Lance's mouth fell open. "April? You smoked dope with this guy?"

April didn't answer, but Tyson flashed a victorious grin. "Hey, man, what's the big deal? It's practically legal in California."

"This isn't California," Lance said. "And I don't do drugs, because I'm not an idiot."

"Man, you of all people need something to chill you out. April told me how messed up things in your family are."

Lance caught his breath and stared at his friend. "April? I told you not to tell anybody!"

Guilt reddened her face. "I'm sorry. I was just worried about you."

"Then you should have done what I said and kept it to yourself." Furious, he got out of the car, slammed the door. He hoped Tyson would just drive away. Lance could call his mom, or he could take the MARTA train back to the stop near Kent's house.

But Tyson got out of the car and followed

him. "Hey, calm down, man. She didn't tell me much."

Lance didn't want to talk to him. "What are you *doing* with her? She's not like the people you hang out with. You trying to turn her into one of your customers?"

Tyson threw his head back and laughed. "Man, you've been watching too much TV."

Lance turned toward him, hands out. "I don't get why you're with her."

"You're jealous!" Tyson said, amused. "Is that it? You want her?"

Lance wanted to deck the guy. "I want to *protect* her from you, even if she does have a big mouth."

Tyson leaned against his car. "Hey, I get what you're going through. Your sister is . . . what? A heroin addict?"

It was none of this guy's business. "I don't want to talk about my sister."

"I'm just sayin', she's all tangled up in some murder, and it must freak you out. They don't arrest people for murder unless they can make a case."

"They did this time."

"Okay," Tyson said, as if trying to calm an angry bear. "I don't blame you for being touchy. And you don't have to worry, man. I think it's really you April digs, not me. Lance this, Lance that. She doesn't even

228

want to go anywhere without you. I think she's just using me for my wheels. That or my weed."

That was enough. Lance turned and headed for the road.

"Come on, dude, climb the tower with me," Tyson said.

"No!"

"All right. Then let's just get back in the car. We're all friends, right? Look at her. She's crying."

Lance turned and looked through the windshield. He didn't want April to cry. His anger faded, and he thought of all that could happen if he left her alone with Tyson. What was next? Cocaine? Would he get her up on that tower?

Anger pulsed through him. Her parents' impending divorce had made her vulnerable, but he thought she had more sense than to get high with a guy like Tyson. It didn't matter how upset she was. Drugs would only make things worse.

She rolled down her window. "Lance, I'm so sorry. I shouldn't have told anybody."

"Got that right," he said. "Maybe if you weren't high you would have kept the secret."

"Can you forgive me for telling him?"

Did she really think he was only mad

about that? "April, you really smoked weed with him?"

Shame twisted her face. "I was depressed. I didn't think it would hurt anything."

"After all I've told you about Emily?"

She got out of the car. "It's not like it's hard drugs."

He couldn't believe he was having this conversation. "You want to wind up like this guy? A high-school junior at nineteen? Every addict started with *something!* They never think it's a big deal."

"Hey, hey," Tyson said, ambling back to his car. "Let's not get personal."

"Personal?" Lance cried. "You don't think it's personal that you're trying to turn her into a dope-head? I'm going home. Come with me, April. We'll take the MARTA."

She glanced at Tyson, then whispered to Lance, "I don't want to hurt his feelings."

Lance couldn't believe her. And to think he'd considered *dating* her. He glanced back at Tyson. He was in the car now, hunched over. What was he doing?

Tyson came out then, his eyes wilder. "Hey, you morons want to know the story about this place?"

April didn't look at him. "Sure."

"This is the place my dad fell from."

Lance stared at him in the darkness.

230

"What? He fell from this tower?"

"Yep."

Lance realized he knew nothing about Tyson's background. Grudgingly, he asked, "Did he survive?"

"Barely. He's a quadriplegic."

"What's that?" April asked. "Paralyzed?"

"From his neck down."

Suddenly interested, Lance looked up at the massive structure. "What happened? Why was he up there?"

Tyson seemed to enjoy the fact that he had gotten their attention. He leaned into the car, turned on his headlights, illuminating the tower. "He was on the crew putting the thing together," he said. "Had all these cranes moving it up there in pieces. He was a welder. He was the one at the top, and when they'd get a section on it, he'd weld the seam to hold it together."

"Sounds dangerous," April said.

"It was. When they got to the part with the catwalk on it, he was standing on that, and when they put the heavy top piece down, it swung . . . just a little. Just enough to knock him off."

Lance's mouth fell open, and he stared at Tyson, stricken. Tyson was smiling, staring admiringly up at the round tank at the top, as if it were some beautiful memory.

April stepped toward him. "Tyson, how long ago was that?"

"Few years. He's still trapped in a wheel-chair." Tyson went to the chain-link fence, climbed over it.

"My mother loved it," he said as he hit the ground on the other side. "She always wanted to lord it over him, and this gave her the chance. He's been at her mercy ever since."

"So . . . why do you come here?" April asked, walking toward the fence. "It must be a horrible memory."

Tyson's eyes seemed to glaze over as he stared up at the tank. "It's the monster that defeated my old man," he said. "So I like conquering it. It means I'm stronger than it is. I climb it every chance I get." He let out a loud whoop. "I'm going up!"

"Your father fell!" April cried. "I don't know how a person could survive that. You'd be crazy to go up there."

"People go up there all the time to service it. I just do it for fun." He pulled a plastic bag of white powder out of his pocket. "And this makes it even more fun."

Cocaine. He was going to snort coke on top of the tower. Tyson laughed at their re-action and stuffed the bag back in his pocket. As they watched him jog to the tower, Lance joined April at the fence. "He's doing coke. Why are you hanging out with this guy?"

"He makes me feel better!" she cried. "My parents are splitting up and I can't handle it. My mom's crying all the time, my dad cusses her out."

"That's no excuse. Just because they're falling apart doesn't mean you have to. What is wrong with you? Why do you want to be like him?"

She brought her hands to her face as Tyson found the ladder attached to one of the columns supporting the tank and pulled himself up like Spiderman scaling a building.

"He's doing it!" she said. "He's gonna fall!"

"Of course he is. He's a lunatic."

Tyson almost faded from sight as he moved farther up, out of the circle of bright illumination. When he reached the top and threw his leg over to the catwalk, Lance brought his hands to his head.

"I can't watch!" April closed her eyes and turned away.

Lance heard Tyson's loud whoop drifting down on the wind, saw him leaning against the rails, arms raised, as if he would launch into flight. Lance went back to the car and turned the headlights on bright, hoping Tyson could see his way down. "I'm calling the police." Lance got his phone out of his pocket and punched in 911.

"Wait! He's coming down." Lance watched through the windshield as Tyson came back to the ladder and backed down it. Lance didn't finish the call.

The tar-like smell of the reefer smoldering in the ash tray was making him sick.

Tyson got to the ground and leaped like a hurdler over the four-foot fence. "Did you see it, babe?" he said to April in a frenzy. "I could *fly* up there. What a rush!"

"You were giving me a nervous breakdown," she said.

"I have stuff to help with that."

Lance shook his head. "No, she doesn't want it. She just wants to go home. We're taking the train. Come on, April."

She got her purse out of the car. "Sorry, Tyson," Lance heard her say.

Tyson only laughed as they walked away. He cranked the music back up, let it blare over the speakers. They could still hear it as they crossed the lanes of traffic to the train station.

CHAPTER 36

Emily was still awake, lying on the couch, when Lance got back to Kent's house. He and April had ridden the train to the stop close to her house, and she'd borrowed her mom's car to bring him home. Kent was already gone.

He wasn't in the mood to talk, but he knew Emily probably needed to. "Hey," he said. "How's your foot?"

"Turning black," she said, moving the ice pack so he could see. "It's killing me. I'm going to the doctor tomorrow to make sure it's not broken."

Lance looked down at it, wincing. It was huge, and the bruise was indeed black. "That looks terrible. You should sue."

"It wasn't the jail's fault. It was that woman." Emily looked up at him then, stared into his eyes. "Are you okay?"

"Yeah," he muttered.

Suspicion narrowed her eyes. "Where'd

you guys go?"

He couldn't look at her. "We just rode around."

For a moment, she was quiet, and he felt like she could see straight through him. "Have you been smoking weed?"

He closed his eyes and sighed. "No."

"Don't lie to me, Lance. I know that when I smell it."

"I said no. I haven't been smoking."

She sat up straighter. "You know you have the same DNA I have. Other people might use drugs and not have a problem, but it didn't take much for me to get addicted. It may not take much for you, either."

Now she was making him mad. "I didn't do it, okay? Just because I was around somebody who was —"

He got up and went to the kitchen area, opened the refrigerator, poured himself a glass of orange juice. When he glanced at her, Emily was staring at him over the back of the couch. "What?" he asked.

"Why were you with somebody who was smoking dope?"

"Because I was trying to protect April. Don't worry. We rode the train home."

"Was she smoking with him?"

There was no point in shading the truth with Emily — she always knew when he was lying. "Not tonight. But she did last night. I knew it wasn't good for her to be alone with him."

"You can't be with her all the time. If she's determined to hang out with a doper, she's going to no matter what."

"But that's just it. He's not just a doper. He deals. I think he's trying to turn her into a customer."

"Could be. Did he offer drugs for free?"

"Yes. She doesn't have any money."

"Lance, stay away from him."

"I plan to. I was thinking of telling Kent. But if he gets arrested or something, he'll know it was me, and we're already in enough danger."

"Tell Kent anyway. If April keeps going with this guy, then she's not the right girl for you."

"But she's just about my only friend. I'm not exactly Mr. Popularity since we moved here. Some of these people have been in school together since they were in kindergarten. They're not that interested in getting to know the skinny dork with the tall tales. She's the only one who is."

"Better to be alone than to get pulled down."

"I know. Mom asleep?"

"Yeah. I told her I'd wait up for you. She's

really tired."

"She probably didn't sleep at all when you were in jail. She was a wreck."

"I know the feeling," Emily said.

He took his glass to the sink, rinsed it out, and put it in the dishwasher. "So get up. Go to bed. That's where I'm sleeping."

"No, I'll sleep with Mom. You get the guest room."

He shrugged. "What if Mom rolls over on your foot? Just take the guest bed. I'm fine on the couch."

"Thanks." She got up and left the blanket, hobbled toward the guest room. Each time she put pressure on her foot, she winced.

"You need crutches," he said.

"Yeah, I've been busy. Hopefully I'll get some tomorrow."

He went to her and let her lean on him, helped her get to the bedroom.

"Thanks, bro. You might want to take a shower before Mom smells that smoke."

"I will."

He showered and changed into shorts and a T-shirt, then stretched out on the couch. As he tried to sleep, he prayed that tonight's episode with Tyson had been enough to keep April from wanting to hang out with the guy again. If she didn't stay away from

Tyson, Lance would have to wash his hands of her, whether he liked it or not.

CHAPTER 37

The twin bed in Kent's guest room was too soft, and Emily tossed and turned all night, kept awake by the searing pain in her foot. Anger that there was no way to relieve it pulsed through her. Tylenol wasn't touching the pain, and she couldn't take anything stronger.

She kept her foot propped on pillows, but that did little good.

By morning, when she put weight on her foot, lightning bolts of pain ratcheted through her, making it impossible for her to think.

She'd been awake for hours when her mother got up.

"I have to go to the doctor," Emily told her. "It hurts so bad I'm thinking maybe it's broken. I can't put any weight on it."

Her mother looked like she could use another couple of hours' sleep. She examined her foot. "I want to go with you, but I

240

can't miss work since I missed yesterday."

"It's okay," Emily said. "I'll go by myself. My right foot is fine, so I can drive."

Emily could see how conflicted her mom was about leaving her to fend for herself, but she was twenty, after all. If she couldn't go to the doctor alone, she really did have problems.

"Just be careful," Barbara said. "That person is still out there." She promised to get her work done quickly, then try to meet Emily at the doctor's. Barbara took the rental car to work and left Emily with her car.

As Emily drove her mother's car to the doctor's office, the unfairness of it all clanged in her head. What did God want from her? Why had he allowed her to be put in this position, experiencing pain that almost debilitated her, from an arrest she didn't deserve?

By the time she reached the clinic, she was sweating with the pain, but the pain ripping at her heart was even worse. God didn't love her, she told herself. He wasn't going to help her.

She sat in the waiting room on the verge of tears, fixated on her emotional and physical pain, and thought how easy it would be to tell the doctor that she needed painkillers. Just one pill would take the edge off her pain. She could keep it down to one. She was different now. She could control herself.

That's a lie. The words flashed through her mind like a neon sign at midnight. She had vowed to live a sober life. She wasn't going to backslide now.

No one ever said sobriety would be easy.

The wait was long and excruciating. She twisted, and propped her foot on the chair next to her, counting down the patients who would go before her. By the time her name was called, she wanted to scream for relief.

First, they did an x-ray. Then she waited in the examining room until the doctor came in to give her the verdict.

He was a skinny, small guy with big ears and big teeth. "Well, I'm glad you came in," he said. "Your foot is definitely fractured."

Great, Emily thought. *What next?* "I was afraid of that. I was hoping it was just a sprain."

"Well, the break doesn't go completely through, so the tendons and ligaments are probably causing most of the swelling and pain." He showed her on the x-ray where she'd cracked the bone.

"We'll give you a boot to wear until the swelling goes down, then we'll cast it. No weight on it at all. And we'll give you something for that pain."

Tell him you can't take narcotics! The urge came from deep inside. It was the Holy Spirit, she knew, giving her an out. If she told the doctor she was an addict, that she'd been in recovery for two years, then he wouldn't give her narcotics to control the pain.

But she said nothing, and he left the room. She stewed over her failure as the nurse wrapped and booted her foot. A battle raged in her mind. Two voices, from opposite regions.

Pain pills will kill the pain and calm your fears.

What did God expect of her, anyway? He could have spared her from the crazy woman who made her twist her foot in the shackles. If he loved her, he would have kept her from being blamed for murder.

Then came the opposing voice: God *was* helping her with sobriety. He'd rescued her from the mire of her choices, and he'd allowed her to be free of jail for now. He expected her to do her part. *Don't move backward. Be the girl he made you to be.*

The doctor came back in and checked the boot. "I want to see you back in a week so we can check the swelling. You'll be in a cast for six weeks."

243

Wonderful. She imagined herself crutching across campus. Or suffering through this inside prison.

"My nurse is getting you crutches. Now remember, don't put any weight on it or you might break that bone clean through."

"Okay. Guess I don't have much choice."

The doctor took a moment to type his notes into his laptop. Then he shook her hand and told her to take care.

No medication. Relief washed over her. No decision to make. But when the nurse came back in with her chart and crutches, she handed Emily a prescription.

Oxycontin.

Emily couldn't speak. *Give it back. Tell her!* But she folded it and slipped it into her jeans pocket.

After checking out, she crutched out to her car. She sat for a moment, staring at the small piece of paper that could have such an impact on her pain and her life. She never should have let this happen.

Did she want to go down this road again?

Pain screamed out, *Yes! It's just so you can think again.* It was nobody else's business. *They* didn't have to hurt.

She'd left herself this open door, and she wanted to go through it. Ignoring the alarms going off in her head, she drove to the nearest Walgreens and left the prescription to be filled. She'd pick it up in an hour.

To kill time, she went to her college campus and sat in the car looking at the football field. She rolled her windows down. Warm wind whipped through her hair.

She should call her sponsor. That was the deal. Whenever she came close to using, she was to get on the phone and talk it out with the woman who'd agreed to walk alongside her in her sobriety. Lana was forty years old and had been sober for fifteen years, after using heroin for ten years — much longer than Emily had.

But she knew what her sponsor would say. Lana, who was a Christian she'd met in her AA group, would tell her to get down on her knees and take it to God. If Emily called her, the door would close.

She didn't want that to happen.

The moment the thought came to her, another one battled it. *Stop this, Emily! You're flirting with your enemy!*

Tears came to her eyes. She tried to pray, but her deception in failing to tell her doctor of her addictions stood between her and God. Why would her creator listen to her about murder or anything else, knowing what she'd done . . . what she was about to do?

Call Lana.

Finally, she summoned the strength to make the call. But she only got Lana's voice mail. No wonder. She was at work. Lana would call her back as soon as she could. But until then . . .

Her heart rate sped up, and perspiration coated her temples. The battle raged in her mind, but this time, she wanted to lose it.

No, she wanted to win. She had to win. Everything depended on it.

She closed her eyes and tried to calm her breathing. What would Lana tell her? She would tell her to force herself to think back through the things she'd done when she was on drugs. The chaos it had brought to her life. The dark doorways it had opened.

With all the strength she had, she forced herself to remember the shame, the desperation, the constant hunger. Arrest . . . jail . . . the disappointment in her mother's eyes. One pill. That was all it would take to open that gateway again. One pill would make her want another one. And then another.

And the last state will be worse than the first. Jesus' words in Luke 11 screeched her thoughts to a halt.

She'd be right back into full-scale addiction within days. All the trust she'd built would be destroyed. Lance would hate her.

She wouldn't be able to defend herself against the murder charges.

Did she really want to go there?

She wilted into tears and looked up at the sky. "God, I hate this! I can't go back to the way I was. But I need your help."

The tears cleansed her, and her admission of weakness gave her an unexpected strength and the certain knowledge that God hadn't forgotten her. He would give her what she needed to get through.

All she had to do was want it.

CHAPTER 38

Word came that morning that Three Roads Baptist Church had accepted their bid. The whole staff was in a festive mood, but Barbara had way too many things on her mind. When the text came from Emily, her mood plunged further.

Foot's broken.

She went into her office and stewed at her desk as anger raged through her. The guards shouldn't have let this happen. Her child, tripped on the stairs, her foot broken in jail! She felt so helpless, so out of control.

Her cell phone rang, and she saw that the readout said Walgreens. Frowning, she clicked it on.

"Hello," an automatic voice said, "this call is to let you know that your prescription is ready for pickup at the Candler Road branch of Walgreens . . ."

Barbara clicked the phone off, her heart rate escalating. Prescription?

This was the number on their family's account. They always called her when any of their prescriptions were ready. *Don't panic.* Emily could have gotten an anti-inflammatory. Just because she had a prescription didn't mean it was for narcotics.

Then she thought of those pills in that FedEx pack, addressed to Emily. She tried to put it out of her mind, but when the questions wouldn't leave her alone, she decided there was one way to find out.

She left the office and drove to the Walgreens near her home, and rolled up to the drive-thru window.

"I have to pick up my daughter's prescription," she told the woman. "Emily Covington." She sat shivering in her car as she waited, cold from dread.

Finally, they came back with the bag. They read out the price, and she handed them her debit card.

Her heart raced as she waited for the drawer to slide out with her card and the bag of pills. Barbara set it beside her and didn't look at it as she drove away. She didn't want the pharmacist to see her reaction. She circled the building and pulled into a parking space. Her breath seemed trapped in her lungs as she tore into the bag and pulled out the bottle of pills.

She spun it in her hand and read the label. Oxycontin.

Her heart plunged into her stomach. What was Emily thinking? Were they about to go through this again?

Her phone rang, and she saw that it was Emily. She didn't want to answer, but anger on the verge of fury prompted her to click it on. "What?" she spouted.

Emily paused. "Uh . . . are you okay? Is it a bad time?"

"It is now," Barbara clipped. "So your foot is broken?"

"Yeah, fractured." Emily was silent for a moment. "I have a boot. Next week I'll get a cast."

"So what are you doing for the pain?" she asked, daring her to lie.

"Tylenol. And I'm supposed to keep it propped up and stay off it until the swelling goes down."

Emily's evasion set a fire inside Barbara. "That all?"

Again, silence. "What's wrong, Mom?"

Barbara breathed a wet laugh, swiped at her tears. "Walgreens called me, Emily. Your Oxycontin is ready to pick up."

Emily's sharp intake of breath made Barbara sick. "I wasn't going to pick it up. I just called them and canceled the order. You must have gotten there before my call."

"And I just rode into town on a hay truck. I know your lies, Emily."

"Mom, don't. Please believe me. I was weak for a minute, I admit, but I prayed and God strengthened me. I wasn't going to get the pills."

"You took it to Walgreens! You had them fill it."

"But I didn't pick it up!"

"You haven't had time!" Barbara shouted.

"Mom, I messed up! I took the prescription to the drugstore, and I shouldn't have. I let myself get weak. But I pulled back. I didn't go through with it. Go inside and ask them. I talked to a girl. I don't know her name, but it was just a few minutes ago."

Barbara hung up without saying good-bye and snatched up the bag. Wiping her tears, she went into the drugstore and stormed to the side window that said DROP OFF.

A female pharmacist stood beside the window, typing on a computer. "Can I help you?" she asked.

Barbara leaned over the counter. "Yes. My daughter is Emily Covington. She just spoke to a woman here."

"Yeah, I talked to her," the pharmacist said. "She said to cancel her order, but after I hung up I realized it had already been picked up."

Barbara closed her eyes, wanting to collapse in relief. So Emily was telling the truth. She had almost fallen, but she had caught herself. *God* had caught her. Wasn't that what mattered?

She told herself it was, but part of her still harbored resentment that Emily would even consider using. As powerful as that pull was, Emily knew how much was on the line. With one decision, their entire world would collapse again.

Barbara went into the store's bathroom and flushed the pills. Then she forced herself to go back to work and get through the rest of the day, though her mind was far away. Anger and relief collided in her head, making it ache. And fatigue over the last few days — and the last few years — were wearing her down.

So much damage. So much fallout. Crazy things happening.

She didn't know how much more she could take.

CHAPTER 39

Barbara was distant when she got back to Kent's after work, so Emily decided to make herself scarce. She had betrayed her mother. She had betrayed herself. The fact that she'd canceled the prescription didn't erase the temporary weakness she'd shown.

She turned to a blank page in her spiral notebook and started journaling.

I'm the black sheep of the family, the problem child, the one everyone dreads and avoids. I'm the one whose future is questionable, the one more likely to wind up in prison than living the good life.

My punishment for my damaged neurons is not over. Broken bones, stalkers, and prison are still on my To-Do list. So much to look forward to. And here I thought my history test was my most pressing issue.

My mother will never trust me as long as she lives. And I guess it's my own fault.

As she hunkered in Kent's small guest room, her school books spread out on the bed, she had to admit that it wasn't just the pain of a broken foot that had weakened her. It was the stress of being falsely accused and the strain of two days in jail. The fear of what might happen next.

So what do I do about this, other than wallowing in self-hatred while I wait for the other shoe to drop?

Her mother had no idea what she was going through. No one did. But that couldn't matter. She had to have integrity regardless of what people thought of her. God was the only one who could help her. Self-pity surely couldn't. She had to figure out how to press on with her goals, and chief among them was to live a righteous life no matter her circumstances.

Abandoning her journal, she opened her Bible, starving for sustenance. She flipped around to the book of Numbers, and turned to the passage where Moses sent twelve spies into the land of Canaan, to bring back a report of the land God had promised. The men came back with a bad report. Ten of them said that the land was flowing with milk and honey, as God had said, but that the people were too big and strong and the cities too well fortified to conquer. "We became like grasshoppers in our own sight, and so we were in their sight."

She could relate. Against her own invisible foe, she was like a grasshopper. One or more killers were jerking her around, manipulating her like a puppeteer, calling the shots on her life. She was as helpless as a grasshopper.

But the negativity of those ten spies in the face of God's promises changed the path of their future. Only Caleb and Joshua trusted God. Despite the practicalities, the fears of the ten other spies, the dangers in taking the land, Caleb and Joshua believed that God would do what he said he would do.

She paused and re-read Numbers 14:9, where the two of them tried to stop the fear and discouragement spreading like cancer through the people. Aloud, she read, "Only do not rebel against the Lord. And do not be afraid of the people of the land, because we will swallow them up. Their protection is gone, but the Lord is with us. Do not be afraid of them."

Maybe that was the word God wanted Emily to hear today. That she need not fear the men who schemed against her. That she was not a grasshopper. That she had the

King of the Universe fighting on her side. Her enemies would be swallowed up. Their protection would be gone. She had nothing to fear.

She prayed that passage of Scripture would apply to her life. The Israelites had rejected God's message and wound up wandering the desert for forty years. She was tired of desert life. She wanted to be like Joshua and Caleb. She wanted to trust God.

Her foot ached, reminding her why she should doubt. She thought of the message the killer had written on the wall of her violated home — *Criss-Cross*. It was just the kind of thing to send her over the edge, and it almost had. Was that what Bo and Carter wanted? To make her a junkie again?

She heard a knock on the door. "Who is it?"

"Me," Lance said. "Can I come in?"

"Sure."

The door opened. Lance looked tired. He must not be sleeping well on the couch. "Are you okay?" he asked.

"I'm fine."

"But . . . why are you and Mom not talking?"

She looked away. "I just needed to be by myself. I'm studying."

Lance looked down at the Bible in front of her. "Studying what?"

"People with integrity." With the word, she burst into tears.

Lance stood there quietly. Finally, he came in and sat on her bed. "Why does that make you cry?"

She shook her head and wiped her face. "Because I want integrity. But it's like I have my old self still strapped to my back, and I just can't shake her off."

"What happened? What did you do?"

She sighed and told him the story. His face fell when she got to the part about taking the prescription to the pharmacy. "Oh, no. Emily."

"I didn't go through with it. I changed my mind before I picked it up, and I canceled it. But Mom found out, and she's pretty upset."

"No wonder."

"Right. No wonder." She wiped her eyes, drew in a deep, cleansing breath. "I'm working on being the kind of person that God can bless. But it's hard because of the choices I made back then. I let myself get caught in this. I put myself there."

"You had a lot of problems, with Dad dying and all."

"So did you. But you made better

choices." She locked her gaze into her brother's, wanting him to understand. "I liked the way the drugs made me feel. And I made decisions . . . one after another . . . decisions that made me lose control. It didn't happen *to* me. I chose it, and then one day I couldn't choose anymore."

"But you did choose. You quit. And even though you almost lost it today, you didn't."

"The thing is, that guy who's been smoking dope in front of you . . . he'll pressure you. You make one decision to use any kind of drug, and the next thing you know, your choices are gone. You think you're immune, that you won't do anything harder. But when you're high, you don't have strong values. You don't have hard rules. You just have your appetite, and you fall for any seduction that comes along."

"Tyson doesn't influence me."

"Not now. But you keep going places with him and he will."

"So now *you're* lecturing *me?* I didn't do anything."

"I know. Just be careful." She knew that jumping on him wasn't necessary. He had his head on straighter than she did.

Suddenly she was tired. So tired. The weight of the last few days was dragging her down. "I didn't kill those women, you know."

He met her eyes. "I never for one second thought you did."

"Anybody knowing my history would question it."

"You're not who you were. End of story." He got up. "I'm hungry. Wonder if there's anything to eat."

Grateful for the period at the end of his sentence, Emily watched him leave, then pressed her face into her hands. No matter what, she had to trust God. She went back to her Bible, searching for the strength and the courage to get through another hour.

CHAPTER 40

Lance couldn't fight his melancholy at school the next day, and when Tyson approached him in the hallway at lunchtime, he had little patience.

"My friend, Lance," Tyson said, thrusting out his fist to bump with Lance. But Lance kept his hand in his pocket. "If I didn't know better, dude, I'd think you don't like me." Humor rippled in his tone.

Lance just kept walking.

Tyson was full of energy, trotting in front of Lance, turning and walking backward. But he looked like death warmed over. His eyes were sunken, like a junkie on a dayslong high, but Lance resisted the urge to push him out of his way.

"What do you want?" Lance asked.

"Just to be friends, man," Tyson said, hitting his own chest and throwing his hands out. "I like you, man. I don't care what the jocks say about you."

"I don't care what they say about me either."

"I looked you up on the Internet. Saw the articles about your shooting. I know it's all true, man."

Lance's steps slowed. It wasn't as if he'd spent a lot of time trying to convince people about what had happened to him back in Jeff City. But when someone acknowledged that it was true, it did him good.

"I've been telling everybody, dude," Tyson said. "You're a cool guy."

Lance stopped walking and stared at him.

"What do I have to do to be your friend?" Tyson asked him.

Lance didn't know what the guy was up to, but he didn't trust him. "Leave April alone."

"Hey, I'm just her friend. You overreacted last night, man. It's not like you caught her shooting crack."

"If you care about her, back off, okay?"

"Hey, you've got problems. If you loosened up, people would like you better. I can hook you up. A little stress reliever to help you forget your sister killed somebody."

Lance's muscles went rigid. "She did *not* kill anybody, so shut your stinkin' mouth."

Again, Tyson's hands came up. "Sorry,

261

man. I didn't say that right. I'm sure she's cool."

"Get out of my way," Lance bit out.

Lance pushed past him. He thought of calling Kent and telling him that a slimy drug dealer was slithering down the halls of the high school. But Tyson was too smart to be caught that way. He wouldn't have more than one hit on him — just enough for a small misdemeanor charge, and he'd be free again within hours. Lance knew how guys like him operated. They kept their stash nearby, in a place that was easy to reach, but never on them. His dopers had to come to a second meeting at a more discreet location to buy from him. He'd never have enough on him to be busted for long.

Brooding, Lance went into the cafeteria. The smell of beef stew assaulted him, making him feel sick. He headed for the salads and found April there.

Her smile almost made him feel better. "Hey, Lance. You okay?"

He shrugged. "Fine."

"So . . . you want to go to Aaron Gray's party tonight?"

He shrugged. Aaron Gray was a basketball player whose parents were millionaires. Lance didn't have a clue why the guy went to public school. The party was for the whole junior class, but Lance hardly knew him. "Not really."

"Come on. It'll be fun."

"I have a lot going on."

He took his tray and headed to an empty table. April followed. "How's Emily?"

"Okay. She broke her foot. Like she needed more bad luck."

"She must be really depressed."

"Yeah. I hope she doesn't have to repeat the semester. But I guess that's the least of her worries."

"Have they caught the killer yet?"

"Nope."

"Then she might really have to go back to jail?" she whispered.

Lance just stared at his food. "Can we change the subject?"

"Yeah. Sure." April took a bite, her soft eyes on him. "Come on and go to the party with me tonight. I don't want to go by myself. It'll get your mind off things."

"Tyson hasn't offered you a ride?" he said sarcastically.

She took the blow. "I don't want to go with him."

"Good." There was hope. He should wash his hands of her for smoking dope with Tyson. But she was weak and down, and Tyson clearly had taken advantage. Maybe

Lance shouldn't be so hard on her.

He drew in a long breath. "Maybe I could get my mom's car."

April's eyebrows shot up. "Really?"

He grinned. "I'll text her and see."

The Grays' house reflected their wealth. Aaron had bragged often about the ten-thousand-square-foot mansion with countless rooms. The party spilled onto the back lawn and around the pool, though it was too cold to swim.

As he and April walked up the drive from where valets had parked his car, Lance's anxiety kicked into hyperdrive. April, who'd grown up here, found friends just inside the house and dashed toward them. Lance stood alone for a moment, then forced himself to head toward the kitchen.

The counters were filled with bottles of everything from Corona beer to Jim Beam. Clearly, the host's parents weren't around . . . or else they had no problem with teenagers getting drunk in their home. Lance found the sodas and poured himself a Coke.

He stepped out of the kitchen and tried to find a place to get out of the way. He missed his friends in Jeff City.

Sitting alone, watching his classmates

drink and dance, he decided that he shouldn't have come. Why had he been so flattered when April asked him? It wasn't like a date. She wasn't paying any attention to him. Maybe she just considered him a project, someone who needed a friend, so she'd made the sacrifice.

He saw a table of food on the back patio and ambled toward it. A couple of people he knew from class stood in front of the chips and salsa. They looked sober and sane, so he went toward them. But as he approached, they walked away. He wasn't sure if they'd seen him and were avoiding him or if they just hadn't noticed. He set his drink down and filled a plate with some chips and dip, then headed for a free chair in a corner of the patio.

As he sat down, he saw Tyson coming in, newly arrived and wild-eyed. He looked worse than he had earlier. Several of Lance's classmates greeted the doper like they'd been waiting for him. He was sure to score big tonight.

Lance sat alone for a while, scanning the crowd for April, but after a while, he re-alized he'd completely lost track of her — and Tyson had disappeared, too. He should just leave, but first he had to make sure she had a ride home. Irritated, he went looking for her. He found one of her friends in the kitchen, mixing rum and Sprite. "Scarlet, do you know where April is?"

"I think they're in the study," she said.

They? Who was *they?*

He crossed the crowded living room toward the foyer, looking for something that looked like a study. A door just off a massive hallway was closed. Maybe that was it.

He opened the door, looked inside at the cluster of people there. A joint was being passed around the circle, its smoke clouding the room.

Lance stepped back, and April shot up. "Lance?"

Lance looked from her to Tyson, who was grinning as he lit another joint and passed it down.

" 'Sup, Lance?" he asked. "Come in and have a toke." His laughter cracked through the room.

Lance ignored him and closed the door. He was outa here. He headed for the front door, but behind him, the study door flew open and April dashed out. "Lance! Don't go."

Lance didn't turn back as he trotted down the steps to the drive.

"Lance! Please wait. I just took one hit."

"I'm going home," he said over his shoulder. He found the car and pulled his keys out of his pocket. "Find a ride."

"No, I'll come with you," she said.

He unlocked the door and April jumped into the passenger seat. "I braced myself for alcohol being here," Lance said, "but I didn't expect dope. I thought you told me it was just a mistake when you did it before, that you weren't gonna do it anymore."

"I know. I'm sorry."

He drove in silence for a moment, unable to look at her. "My sister started with things like this, you know. And then one day at a party just like that one, somebody handed her a pill and said, 'Take it. It'll make you feel better.' So she took it and it calmed her, and she thought that was her answer. She could be a big party girl, do whatever she wanted, have so much fun, if she would just get high before she went. But you know what happened? Before she knew it, she wasn't taking it because it made her feel good. She was taking it because if she didn't she would puke her guts out. And she spent every minute of the day trying to figure out where she was gonna get her next hit. And then the pills stopped being enough. So she started using heroin and cocaine and anything else she could get her hands on. She threw my mom and me under the bus and lost all her friends."

April stared at him in the darkness.

"My mother raised her with perfect teeth, and now she has fourteen fillings in her mouth. She'd hang out in rat holes of apartments and dope houses, shooting poison into her veins. It all started as no big deal. Just one hit. One joint. One pill."

April set her elbow on the window and let out a long breath. "I know you've seen some bad stuff. But I've been really depressed about my parents, and I just wanted to feel better."

"You think you got problems? My friend Jordan was a second-generation meth addict. Her mother traded Jordan's baby for drugs, and Jordan and her baby almost died. People like her and my sister are fighting for their lives every day, and you have the stupidity to flirt with it like it's no big thing. I can't hang out with you, April. I was gonna ask you to homecoming, but I don't want to anymore."

She turned her rounded eyes to him. "Really? You were? I would've said yes."

That didn't make him feel better. "I should save my money anyway. Trying to buy a car."

She wiped her face. He fought the disappointment surging through him. She was his only friend, and he hated being alone.

But he'd had enough stupidity in his life. Best to move on now, while he had a choice.

CHAPTER 41

It was all Kent could do to stay out of Emily's case. Professionalism dictated that he leave things to Andy and Strand, but when he heard them discussing it in the office, he couldn't help weighing in.

"I just got a call from the print tech," Andy was saying. "He says the pill bottle Kent bagged at the Covington house didn't have any prints on it but Kent's."

"None?" Strand asked. "Not even Emily's?"

"Nope. Said it looked like it was polished clean."

"I didn't expect Emily's prints," Kent said from across the room. "Emily didn't touch it. But why wouldn't it have any prints at all, even from the pharmacist?"

"Pharmacist was probably wearing gloves."

"But wiped clean? That's not likely. Someone would have touched that bottle."

"You're not on the case, Harlan," Strand said. "We've got this."

"I'm just sayin'. That's the kind of thing someone who planted that bottle in her house would've done. Her name was on the bottle, so why would Emily bother to wipe her prints but not hide her name . . . or hide the bottle, for that matter? It doesn't add up. But it does add up that the guy who broke into her house and wrote on the wall and stole her necklace could have left the bottle."

Strand leaned back in his chair, hands clasped behind his head. "Hey, Kent? We get it. You don't think she did it."

"I see her all the time," he said. "She's sober and rational. Even if she had some reason to commit these crimes, she wouldn't be stupid enough to leave pills out on her counter and a necklace at the crime scene. If you considered that possibility, then you'd start looking at people who have it in for her. Maybe others at Haven House where she works — somebody who knew about that movie and heard that conversation. *Criss-cross* is a huge clue . . ."

"Let us do this, Kent," Andy cut in. "Trust me, man. We've worked together a long time. You know I'm thorough."

Yes, Andy was thorough . . . sometimes.

But he could miss obvious things. Kent got the Rolaids out of his drawer. Throwing two into his mouth, he prayed they would listen.

Chapter 42

He had never had more fun. Power and invincibility surged through the Avenger's veins with the rapid beat of his heart. He'd gotten away with everything, as though he were invisible, stealing around like a spirit . . . like a god.

He had taken control of his destiny and the destiny of others, and he had so much more to do. So many people who deserved his vengeance.

His mind raced with possibilities. He couldn't rest just yet. There was more . . . there was Emily.

She'd thought moving to that cop's house would protect her, but he knew where she was. She'd been intent on protecting others from him at Haven House. Now they'd see if she could protect her family.

He sped down the road with no worries of police pulling him over. He was all powerful. They couldn't see him. He was like a shooting star, like a meteorite hurling toward an unsuspecting target. When he was ready to wreak more havoc on Emily and her family, they wouldn't be able to stop him. He defied all laws . . . all senses.

As he drove, he inhaled the crack in his bong pipe, felt it shooting through his synapses, igniting every nerve fiber.

He could do anything, and he could do it now. No one could stop him.

CHAPTER 43

By the time she was ready for bed, Barbara's head ached with fatigue and the tears she'd shed. She'd expected Kent to come by tonight and get some clothes before going over to baby-sit her house, but he hadn't come. He'd had to work on a case. She hadn't been able to share her anxiety over the incident at Walgreens. It had left her off-balance and confused. Yes, Emily had canceled the order for the drugs. But the fact that she'd considered buying them, and had almost gone through with it, scared Barbara to death.

Now having Kent off the case left her a raw bundle of nerves. He'd slept the last four nights at her house, and of course nothing had happened while he was there. But it was just a matter of time. Would the murderer kill Emily next time? Would he plant more evidence to make her look guilty? Or were these all just signs of Emily falling apart?

Maybe Barbara was in denial about her daughter's state of mind. Did she want to believe in Emily's sobriety so badly that she ignored the obvious? Staying out late, secrecy, crazy outlandish stories that might or might not be true . . .

What would she do if Emily really was using again? Maybe she only canceled the prescription after she realized she'd be found out.

If Emily was using, Barbara would have to put her out of the house. She couldn't have her influencing Lance or bringing drugs into their home.

But how could she do that — throw her out onto the street and leave her to her own devices? She only had a part-time job. And there was school . . .

She closed her eyes, asking God what he would demand of her next. Friends from her Jeff City support group had been forced to cut their children off after they'd refused to give up drugs. They struggled with Jesus' teachings about giving to those who ask, turning the other cheek, forgiving seventy times seven, giving their children fish instead of a stone. But sometimes withholding help was a fish, when refusing to support them could be the pivotal point that brought change.

How would Barbara make such a decision if it came to that?

Barbara pictured Satan slithering nearby like Gollum, whispering thoughts into her ear to throw her daughter under the bus. He would delight in their suffering. It was just the kind of thing he did. He would love to use some addict who'd snapped to terrorize their family. Already they couldn't live safely in their home. What else would he take from them?

She heard a car in the driveway. Lance had come home twenty minutes ago and gone back to Emily's bedroom to watch TV. Barbara went to the window and saw Kent getting out of his car. Her anger at him for taking himself off the case reared its head in her again. He could have helped Emily. He could have made sure she didn't get blamed for Devon Lawrence's murder.

Now they were at the mercy of his partner and some new guy who was anxious to make his mark.

Kent came in the side door from the garage and smiled at her. Though she didn't want to smile back, she couldn't avoid the warmth that filled her when he was around.

"Hey," he said, coming closer and touching her face.

She took his hand, closed her eyes, and accepted his touch.

"I like coming home to you," he said.

She pulled away and turned to the dishes in the sink. "I thought you were coming earlier."

"Yeah, well. There was a shooting tonight. I had to take the case. But we have the guy in custody, and three witnesses to tell the story, so I didn't have to stay all night." He leaned against the counter, watching her. "Barbara? Look at me."

She turned to him.

"What's wrong?"

"What's *wrong?*" she asked. "Uh . . . well, my daughter's life is hanging by a thread, her foot is broken, and there's a murderer stalking us . . ."

"I know all that."

"Well, what you don't know is that Emily came within an inch of buying drugs today."

She hadn't wanted to tell him. It made Emily look guilty. He wouldn't understand. *She* didn't understand.

His expression fell and he came toward her, reaching for her. "Don't," she said, but she didn't pull away. "I'm mad at the world right now. Emily . . . you . . ."

"I know," he whispered, kissing her hair. "But let me hold you for a minute. Then you can yell at me."

She fell against him and wept into his shirt, letting out her grief and stress, her anxiety and fear. He made things so right. Even when she didn't want him to, even when she was angry, his very presence comforted her.

"I'm sorry I wasn't here earlier," he said.

She whispered a laugh. "Yeah, and I'm sorry some guy got killed."

She looked up and saw the love in his eyes. She *could* talk to him, even about her fears with Emily. He wasn't on the case. Maybe that was how God was working here. "So tell me about Emily," he said.

She drew in a long, weary breath. "Today Emily went to the doctor and he gave her a prescription for Oxycontin. She almost got it filled."

"Almost?"

"She took it to Walgreens."

He led her to the couch, pulled her down next to him, and listened as she unloaded. Finally, when she'd finished, he said, "Emily's all right, Barbara. She's going to have those times, and I think God let you see this one so you could be assured that she can make the right decisions."

"But I'm so mad at her for thinking that way right in the middle of all this mess."

"This mess is *why* she was thinking that way. The whole thing encourages me, if you want to know the truth."

She wiped her wet face. "Really? It doesn't make you think those pills you found on the counter were hers?"

"Nope. Her fingerprints weren't even on the bottle or the envelope. Her name was, but not her prints. The guy who left that bottle wiped it clean. They weren't Emily's. But the fact that he left them there is a big clue. Andy and Strand are on it."

"But I wish *you* were on it."

"I'm not officially on it, babe. But I haven't left you high and dry. I'm still piecing it together. Still adding things up. And I'm telling them everything that comes to me. The main thing is that you're safe here."

She leaned her head on his shoulder. "I should be counting my blessings instead of getting consumed by fear. Emily's okay, and we have you. Things will work out. They have to."

She wanted him to agree with her, to say that everything would be okay. But he didn't.

"Where are the kids?" he asked finally.

"Emily's in bed. She's kept a low profile tonight. I know she's mad at herself."

"And Lance?"

"He got home early from the party he went to with April. He's watching TV."

Kent glanced toward the bedrooms. The light was still on in Emily's room. "Can I go talk to them?"

She shrugged. "Sure."

He kissed her forehead, then got up and knocked lightly on Emily's door. "Emily, it's Kent. Can I come in?"

"Okay," she said.

He opened the door and stepped inside. She lay on the bed with her Bible in her lap, her booted foot propped on a pillow. Lance was sprawled on the floor, leaning back against the wall. "Sorry about your foot, Emily."

"It's okay," she said. "I'll live."

He came in and lowered to a bench by the wall. "How was your day, Lance?"

He shrugged like he didn't want to talk. "Had better."

"Haven't we all?" Kent looked back at Emily. "Hey, Emily, I want you to know I'm proud of you."

She shot him a look like he'd said something absurd. "Proud?"

"Yeah. You chose the right thing today. I know it must have been hard. But I'm proud of what you did."

She blew out a disbelieving laugh. "Did

281

you tell Mom that?"

"Just did."

She gave him a weak smile. "Thanks."

"Don't beat yourself up about it, okay? You're gonna be fine."

"Yeah, if I don't go to prison."

Lance spoke then. "This guy . . . whoever he is. He's not smart. He's been taking a lot of chances. He's gonna mess up and expose himself."

"I think so too," Kent said.

He spoke with the kids for a few more minutes, but it was clear they weren't in chatty moods, so he went back to Barbara. She was standing in the hall, listening. As he came toward her, she smiled and stroked his stubbled face. "Thank you," she whispered.

He kissed her then and she didn't recoil. He thought of the ring in his pocket. Maybe he shouldn't wait. Maybe the time was never going to be perfect. Maybe tonight was the right time . . .

But outside, he heard the deep rumble of a car engine, slowing . . . stopping in front of the house. A car door closed.

Barbara pulled back and looked toward the front door. "Is someone here?"

He went to the window and peered out. A dark four-door sedan he didn't recognize sat idling along the curb in front of his house, silhouetted by the street lamp.

He searched the yard. No one was coming to the door. Where was the driver?

Alarm bells rang in his mind. Quickly, he drew his weapon from his shoulder holster. "Barbara, something's not right. Go to the kids. Lock the bedroom door."

Her eyes rounded with terror. "But who is it? Do you think — ?"

"I don't know. I can't see him. Go, Barb. Call 911 and tell them to send some backup."

She grabbed the cordless phone and ran with it.

Dragging in a deep breath, Kent opened the front door quietly, keeping the porch light off. Clutching his gun, he stepped out into the yard.

Barbara raced to the guest room as she dialed 911. "Kids, get down on the floor!" She didn't know what good that would do, but they had to do something.

They both just sat there as she locked the door and dragged a chair in front of it, wedged it under the doorknob.

"What is it?" Emily asked.

"Now!" Barbara cried. "Down! Someone's out there!"

Lance got up and lunged for the window. Barbara grabbed her son's shirt and jerked him down as Emily awkwardly moved off the bed.

The dispatcher answered. "911 operator."

"Yes, Detective Kent Harlan's house. 552 Dunbar Street. Please hurry!"

"Ma'am, what is your emergency?"

"Someone's here . . . we saw a car and he's in the yard . . ."

"Is he trying to break in?"

It was too complicated to tell her that she didn't know what he was doing, but that it could be the stalker trying to murder them. "Yes," she said simply. "Please . . . hurry. Kent's out there. He needs help!"

Emily started to cry, and Barbara got on the floor and held her as she listened for the next disaster.

In the dark yard, Kent heard liquid splashing on the side of the house, then a whooshing sound.

The car was still there, idling empty on the street. He cornered the house, his weapon raised. The smell of fire and gas almost choked him. As he hit the backyard, he saw flames climbing the back wall.

A car door slammed.

He raced back around to the front. The

car was pulling away. In the darkness, he saw a blotch on the back right fender — a dent, maybe, or a patch of Bondo — but he couldn't see who was behind the wheel or the tag on the car.

Barbara!

He bolted back in. "Barbara, get out! The house is on fire! Hurry!"

The door flew open, and Barbara and both kids came out in a huddle.

"Outside! He's gone, but he set the house on fire."

"How'd he know where we were?" Emily cried. "Nobody knew!"

They all followed Kent outside, Emily hopping on one foot as they stepped into the smoke-filled yard. "The cars!" Emily shouted.

She was right — if the flames reached them, they would explode. But there was no time to move them, and Kent didn't have Barbara's keys. He'd left his own on the counter. He grabbed the water hose, cut it on full-blast, and sprayed the flames. By now the fire had spread across the whole back wall of the house.

He heard Barbara calling 911 again as he tried to fight the flames.

Within a couple of minutes, sirens wailed over the neighborhood, growing louder.

When the engines stopped in front of his house, he filled the firemen in as they dragged their hoses to the blaze.

"It was arson," he shouted, out of breath. "He left a gas can over there. Don't touch it. We need to process it for prints."

Police cars began arriving, and he rushed out to them. Sucking in smoky air, he told the story again. Andy and Strand pulled up finally, along with a CSI. They put out an APB on the car. Hopefully some uniformed officer would find the arsonist and pull him over.

Kent sat out on the curb with Barbara and the kids as the fire department worked on his house.

As the long night wore on, crime scene techs logged the gas can as evidence, and Kent made sure they made molds of the footprints they'd found in the dirt. They blocked off the street and lit up the house and yard with floodlights as police searched the yard for more clues to the arsonist's identity.

Structurally, the house was okay. The fire had been put out in time. Kent hoped the interior of the house would still be fit to live in, but the firemen told him there was too much smoke and fire damage in the back part of the house.

More than likely, this had been another attempt on Emily's life. But how had the killer known where she was?

He paced, enraged, watching the efforts being made to put out any smoldering sparks in his house. The flames were out now, but what was untouched by the fire was damaged by smoke. This killer was tormenting Emily and her family, bent on her eventual death. He must be insane. He was fixated on a goal, and he wasn't going to rest until he'd achieved it. He had to be stopped.

Kent thought of Bo and Carter. The police could easily find out if either drove a dark four-door sedan and if they had alibis at the time of the attack. Both men had priors, so their fingerprints could be compared to the ones on the gas can — assuming there were any.

But Kent couldn't wait for that information. He had to act now . . . tonight . . . before this person struck again. He would get to the bottom of this himself.

Tonight he would find out once and for all who was to blame.

CHAPTER 44

When the fire was out and the fire department had left a small crew there to watch the smoldering debris, Kent took Barbara and the kids to a hotel and checked them in. With a maniac on the loose, they couldn't go back home. He rented a room for himself next door to them and tried to sleep, but rage pounded through his veins, throbbing in his head. He had to know whether Bo drove a dark four-door sedan. He got on the phone and got the dispatcher to check on the make and model of both Bo's and Carter's cars.

Bo's was a 2000 Maxima, dark gray. It could have been the same car. Carter drove a pickup truck, but his dead wife had a burgundy Altima.

He wondered if Bo had been at work tonight. If he smelled like booze, gasoline, and smoke.

Kent's clothes still smelled of smoke, but

he didn't care. He loaded his weapon, holstered it, and pulled his jacket over it. Then he slipped out of his room, careful not to let Barbara hear in the room next door.

"Where you going?"

Lance's voice startled him. Kent spun around and saw the boy sitting on the floor in the hall. "Lance — why are you out here?"

"I was talking to April on the phone. I didn't want to wake up Mom and Emily."

"Go back in. Your mother might wake up and get scared."

"I know," he said. "But that stupid doper Tyson showed up at her house again. She said she'd call me right back. I'm waiting."

Kent could see the pain on Lance's face. "Well, don't wait much longer, okay?"

"Okay," Lance said. "Where are you going?"

"I can't sleep. I thought I'd go take care of a few things."

"About Emily's case?"

He didn't want to lie to Lance. "Sort of."

"Want me to go with you?"

The innocent question moved him. "Not tonight."

Lance's phone chimed as Kent got on the elevator.

The drive to Bo Lawrence's house, where

289

Kent had worked the scene of Devon's murder, took twenty minutes across town. In this lower-income neighborhood, men loitered on corners. He slowed as he passed them, wondering if one of them could be his culprit.

There were flower bouquets around a cross on the front lawn of the Lawrence house. There was no light in the windows.

His headlights lit up a car in the driveway. It was an older model sedan, all right. Dark, four doors. It seemed bigger than the one Kent had seen at his house tonight, but then, he'd been stressed at the time, probably not as observant as he habitually was. And it didn't have a dented fender. Maybe he'd imagined that or the streetlights had cast shadows.

He slowed in front of the house, wondering if Bo smelled like gasoline and whether his tennis shoes matched the pattern they'd found in the yard. He couldn't barge into Bo's house and insist on smelling the guy.

Still . . . he had to know. He pulled his car into the driveway and went to the door. No answer, and no sounds inside. Either he was hiding, sleeping, or he'd gotten a ride somewhere.

He went back to his car. If by some chance Bo was at work, he could easily walk into his store and confront him. He had to find out. He pulled out of the driveway, suddenly sure what he had to do. He drove around for a few minutes, making a plan.

His heart hammered. His head pounded.

He turned around and headed to Bo's convenience store. It wasn't far from where Bo lived. He thought of the morning that he'd gone in and told the guy his wife was dead. He'd truly seemed surprised and grief-stricken. But the man could be a good actor.

Kent pulled into a parking space in front of the store, peered in through the barred windows.

There sat Bo behind the counter, talking to a co-worker. Kent quelled the urge to run inside, grab him by the collar, and shake the truth out of him. *You trying to kill people I love? Trying to destroy my home?*

That would be stupid. He had to be professional.

He set his chin, pulled his lips tight, and got out of the car. Quietly, he closed his door. He didn't delude himself into thinking Bo would confess, but maybe he could trip him up.

He pushed open the glass door and stepped into the store. Bo's back was to him, but his co-worker looked up at Kent.

"How ya doin'?"

Kent didn't answer, just strode toward the counter.

Bo turned around and looked startled to see him. "Hey, Detective."

Kent's lips were so tight he could hardly speak. "Criss-cross," he said.

Bo stared at him. "What?"

Kent didn't repeat it. "How long have you been here tonight, Bo?"

Bo took a step back. "What's going on?"

Was that smoke he smelled? Something in his chest snapped. "I asked you a question. How long have you been here tonight?"

"Okay, I've been here since seven o'clock. This guy's been with me the whole time."

The co-worker, who looked about seventeen, nodded. "Yeah, man. No lie. He's been here all night."

Bo's intense gaze was almost convincing. "What's going on? Did something else happen? Other police were here earlier tonight, asking me questions, but they wouldn't say why."

So Andy and Strand had already been here. Kent stood there, his chest heaving. Had they confirmed Bo's alibi?

Kent closed his hands into fists. "I saw your car at my house. The one sitting in your driveway."

"My car ain't been out of the driveway in two days. I have a flat and haven't had time to change it. Go back and look!"

Kent set his chin. "Your shoe. Take it off. I want to see it."

Bo twisted his face as if he thought Kent was crazy, but he slid his tennis shoe off and handed it to him across the counter.

Kent turned it over. The pattern wasn't like the one he'd seen in the yard. That had had more of a bull's-eye pattern. This one had a grid pattern with horizontal lines.

Maybe it wasn't him.

Bo took his shoe back. "The person who killed Devon . . . he's still doing stuff, ain't he?"

Kent just stared at him.

Bo leaned on the cash register. "Maybe Carter did all this — killed Devon . . . came to your house." His voice cracked, and he looked like he struggled to hold back tears. "Look, man, I know I trashed her while I was in treatment. I said things. But when I got home, things were better. I was sober, and the kids really liked it, and Devon and I were going to free counseling at this church she found. We were trying to get help. But then, somebody came into my house and murdered her . . ."

"How did you know about Cassandra?"

293

"Are you kidding?" Bo said. "The police have interviewed me over and over. They wanted my alibi." Bo broke down then, his mouth twitching. "So if Carter did this . . . if he killed Devon and Cassandra . . . he must have relapsed and gone off the deep end. But he *never* called me. I ain't talked to him since rehab."

If that was true, Carter's actions didn't make sense. Why would he kill Bo's wife? There was nothing in it for him, even if he was high.

"Let's go see him," Bo said. "Right now. I can't go in my car until I can fix my tire. But we could go in yours."

The co-worker nodded. "Head out, man. I would if I was you. I'll hold down the fort."

Was this a trick? Kent knew his anger dulled his professional reasoning skills. He had to get a grip.

"You're a cop," Bo said. "You're armed. I'm the one who should be afraid to go with you. But no lie, I want to confront Carter."

Kent's chest was so tight he thought it might burst. "I just want to see his car."

"Fine. But go back and look at mine," Bo said. "It ain't been nowhere, man. It's also got a hole in the radiator, so even before the tire went flat, I couldn't drive it far."

Kent didn't want to believe him, but he

couldn't walk away. He just stared at Bo.

"Man, if there's a chance that Carter killed Devon, I want to know," Bo said. "Whoever did it changed my life. My kids are suffering. Now I have to raise 'em by myself without their mama. Her parents are tryin' to get custody, because they don't trust me to stay sober. Can't blame 'em. I don't trust *myself*. And there's no way Emily Covington did any of this."

Kent felt suddenly fragmented, not sure what to do next. His house was uninhabitable. The people he loved were displaced, and their lives were still in jeopardy. The person doing all this was getting sloppy, taking risks. Why, then, was it so hard to prove who it was?

"Come on, man," Bo said. "Let's go see Carter. If he did it, I'll be able to tell. I know the guy. His emotions show on his face, and I know what he looks like when he lies. He can't hide it from me if he did it. If he's the one, I'll testify against him."

If Kent had been assigned to the case, he would never consider something so unprofessional. But now he was just a victim, fighting for the lives of the people he loved. He considered Bo, standing there with lines of grief and fatigue on his face, waiting for the word.

Bo couldn't be the arsonist if he'd truly been here all night. And when Cassandra was killed, it was highly unlikely that Bo could have pulled it off, when Kent had spent so much time with him that day.

It had to be Carter. There might be evidence in his car. His phone might have tracked where he'd been tonight. Kent had to know, and if he was right, then he could get Andy and Strand to make an arrest. He doubted seriously that they'd gone to Birmingham tonight in search of his arsonist. He couldn't make an arrest without a warrant, but he could question the man, look through the windows of his car.

He let out a long sigh. "All right," he said. "Let's go."

Bo gave a few instructions to his friend, then followed Kent out to his car.

As Kent pulled out of the parking lot with Bo next to him, he prayed he wasn't making a mistake.

CHAPTER 45

Before they left town, Bo insisted they drive by his house so he could prove his tire was flat. He'd gotten a ride to work, he said, and hadn't driven since yesterday. Just as he'd said, the tire was flat, and the engine was cold.

Kent should have noticed that, he thought, but his emotions had been leading. Just one more reason Kent had been right to remove himself from the case.

As they drove to Birmingham, Bo talked about what he'd been through since getting out of rehab.

"I wasn't serious then," he admitted. "I didn't go to rehab because I wanted to. I was forced to. And the whole time I was in there I was determined not to give my mother and my wife and the government what they wanted. They could force sobriety on me while I was there, but I was just biding my time until I could get out and go right back to it."

"Not a good recipe for long-term sobriety."

"Yeah, well. After Carter got out, when I had nobody my age to shoot the breeze with, I started seeing what a fool all them dopers were. They were getting pretty wild, most of them. No intentions of getting better. Just trying to work the system. I'd been using since I was fifteen. And there I was at forty. I didn't want to act like those stupid kids who saw themselves as party animals. They were really ruining their lives."

Kent was quiet. He thought of Emily and what a tremendous journey she'd made from addiction to sobriety. Staying there had been an even greater achievement.

"There was this dude there named Jack. Constantly smuggling in dope. Judge sent him to rehab, but it didn't do no good. Finally got thrown out. I couldn't stand that guy. He had serious mental problems, always accusing us of dissin' him, stirring up trouble where there wasn't any. Paranoid. Had fried his brain, and was almost as bad sober as he was when he was high. But he stayed high most of the time, even there. I didn't want to be like that. By the time I got out, I had an AA sponsor lined up. I've worked the program since I got home."

"Did you tell Devon you wanted to stay clean?"

Sorrow changed his face. "Yeah, I told her, but she didn't believe me. I figured when she saw changes in me, she'd get excited. I started to see that she was tryin' to save our family and our kids from a loser father. She wasn't the bad guy. I was."

Kent glanced at Bo as he drove. Headlights briefly illuminated his face, and there were tears glistening in the man's eyes. He couldn't know for sure, but Bo looked sincere.

"So you've been sober ever since rehab?"

"Yeah, I have. Not that it's been easy. After what happened . . ." His voice broke off. "I started to think it wasn't worth it . . . that I couldn't be expected to stay sober with all this going on. But my little girl said, 'Daddy, who's gonna take care of us?' I told her I would, and she said, 'Daddy!' Like that was ridiculous. Like I was so irresponsible that nobody could expect me to step in and take over."

"So you didn't relapse?"

"No. My AA sponsor talked sense into me."

Calling a sponsor was a decision in itself. Most addicts didn't want to make that call when they were craving. They'd made their minds up to use before there was even a struggle.

On the other hand, maybe nothing Bo said was true.

They were quiet for the next several minutes, then Bo said, "Detective, tell me you believe me, man. Tell me you don't think I killed my wife. That you know I didn't try to burn your house down."

Kent clenched his molars, felt the tightening in his temples. He hesitated. "It doesn't matter what I believe," he said finally.

Bo accepted that. "What could Carter be thinking? He knew I was joking about swapping murders. The next day we laughed about it. He said, 'If we stay in this place much longer we'll scheme to kill our wives, our parents, our cousins . . .' And I said, 'Yeah, we'll even be plotting to kill the president. As if slackers like us could ever pull that off.' And we cracked up because it was totally ridiculous."

"Maybe that started Carter thinking."

"I never woulda thought so." Bo sighed. "So what do we do when we get there?"

Kent didn't answer. He wasn't sure yet.

He'd love to kick down the door and drag him out of his house, smash his face in, tie him up and make an arrest.

When they reached Birmingham, Kent

programmed the address into his GPS. As he waited for it to give him the directions, he wondered if he was doing the right thing. Here he was, in the middle of the night, doing police work on a case that wasn't his, with one of the persons of interest in the car with him.

He must be losing it.

But someone had tried to kill Emily for the second time, and Barbara and Lance along with her. They had torched his own house. He couldn't just sit around waiting for the guy to succeed.

"I want to talk to him," Bo said. "I want to go to the door and look into his eyes."

Kent thought about that. If he knocked on the door, showed Carter his badge, and asked to interview him, would that fly? No. He wasn't on the case. He could get suspended for pulling a stunt like that. And when an arrest was made, his attorney would use that breach in policy to get him off. "No, we can't do that."

The calm, female GPS voice directed him to "follow the highlighted route." When they reached Carter's neighborhood, Kent's heart rate sped up.

There were no lights on at Carter's house, but two vehicles sat in the driveway. A pickup truck and Cassandra's car. Yes, the car could have been the one he'd seen tonight, but he couldn't see the back right fender.

He turned off his lights and pulled to the curb. Killing his engine, he sat for a moment, staring toward the house.

Carter had had plenty of time to get home after his attack. He could be sleeping it off by now.

Kent reached under the seat for his flashlight. "Stay here," he said. "I want to look at that car."

Bo did as he was told. Kent closed the door gently. It clicked, but not loudly enough to wake anyone. He headed up the driveway toward the sedan closest to the side door of the house.

A motion light flashed on in the carport as Kent reached the car.

And then he saw something.

Feet . . . blood . . .

He drew his weapon and stepped closer.

A man lay slumped in a pile, a bullet's gaping exit wound in his back.

Bending over, Kent took the man's pulse. Dead.

The man looked like Carter Price.

His heart sprinted as he looked around for anyone waiting in the shadows. No one was there. Kent backed away and headed to

302

his car, pulling out his phone.

Bo's door came open. "Was the car warm?"

Kent didn't answer. His hand was shaking as the Birmingham 911 Dispatcher answered. "I need police at 9340 Sharon Drive," he said. "There's a dead man in the carport."

CHAPTER 46

"You're sure it's Carter?" Bo asked, stunned as they waited for the police at Kent's car.

"Pretty sure. I've seen pictures."

"Can't I go look?"

"No. You need to stay back."

Bo rubbed his face. "Who did this? If Carter wasn't the killer, who *is?*"

Kent couldn't make sense of it either. Bo was shivering, his breath coming hard. "Come on," Kent said. "Let's sit in the car." He could hear sirens some distance away.

Bo opened the door, dropped into the seat. "What's going on? First Devon, then Cassandra, now Carter?"

Blue lights flashed up the street as the sirens grew louder. From both directions, police cars and ambulances arrived, parking on the street. Kent went to meet them.

As the first cop came toward him, Kent showed his badge and told them what he'd found. The motion-detecting light had gone

304

out, leaving the body invisible from where they stood. "I'm pretty sure it's Carter Price," he told them. "He's been shot dead."

The other officers went past him, and Kent hung back with Bo, standing next to his car door, the window rolled down.

"Gotta be somebody we knew at Haven House," Bo muttered. "Nobody else knows all three of us — me, Carter, and Emily. It's the only thing we all have in common."

Kent stared toward the house. "But who? Was there somebody there who had it in for all of you?"

"I don't know," Bo said. "I mean, I wasn't there trying to make friends. But I never thought I made enemies."

"Did Carter or Emily?" Kent asked.

Bo stared vacantly into darkness. "That Jack dude. Emily caught him bringing drugs back in after we told her he had them. She turned him in. He got kicked out. Had to go back to jail."

"Jack," Kent repeated. "The guy you said was crazy?"

"Yeah. That guy."

Kent lifted his eyebrows. "Do you think he could have heard you and Carter talking about your wives?"

Bo was silent for a moment. "He could have. He was in and out."

Kent pulled out his notebook and got his pen. "Bo, what was Jack's last name?"

"Tyson," Bo said. "His name was Jack Tyson."

Chapter 47

Lance should have washed his hands of April, but her texts and calls about Tyson had riled him, and he'd spent two hours sitting in the hotel hallway, trying to talk her into staying away from him. Then the guy had shown up at her house and April told Lance she'd call him back.

Sick, he'd gone back into the hotel room and tried to sleep, putting his phone on silent, but thoughts of her smoking dope with Tyson, and maybe doing worse, along with all the things that had happened tonight, kept him awake like he'd guzzled Red Bull.

Then his phone vibrated, and he went into the bathroom and snapped up the call. "April?" he whispered so he wouldn't wake his family.

He heard a yelped scream, then sobbing broken by a bad connection. "Lance . . . tower . . . please help!"

Lance slipped back into the hallway, careful to close the door quietly behind him. "April? April, I can't hear you!"

The phone call cut out; he'd lost the connection. His mind raced. If Tyson was taking her back to the tower, she could be in real danger. He had to rescue her from the insanity of this doper who wouldn't leave her alone. Maybe now she'd listen. Maybe she'd never use drugs again.

He slipped back in and got his mother's keys off the dresser. Neither his mother nor Emily woke up as he went out.

From the parking lot, he texted April — *On my way.*

He hoped the threat of his coming would settle Tyson down.

Lance prayed as he drove.

CHAPTER 48

The name hit Kent like a lead ball. Tyson? Jack's name was *Tyson?* Wasn't that the name Lance had mentioned tonight?

"But that stupid doper Tyson showed up at her house. She said she'd call me right back. I'm waiting."

Could it be the same guy?

If Tyson was the same person who was making a move on Lance's girlfriend . . . Kent's heart stumbled. "So Emily is the one who got him kicked out?" he asked Bo. "What happened?"

"They arrested the guy right there, and he screamed like a hyena all the way out. He went to jail for a few months."

Something exploded in Kent's chest. "You didn't bother to tell me that before?"

"I didn't think of it until just now, man!"

Kent pulled out his phone. Should he call Andy or Barbara first? Lance had to know this now. This explained how the killer knew the Covingtons were staying at his house instead of their own. He could have followed Lance there from school . . . or maybe Lance let it slip.

Bo's words came faster now. "Jack, he had a nightmare mother — controlling and mean — and his dad was in a wheelchair. He was a brick shy of a load, I'm telling you. Scary dude."

Terror clutched him. Was Tyson baiting Lance to cause more chaos for Emily?

So what would Tyson do now? If his insanity had escalated to the point that he'd start a fire and murder someone else the same night, after already killing two others, would he just sit by and wait to hear about his accomplishments on the news? Or would he be agitated enough to do more?

Kent speed-dialed Barbara's phone.

Barbara jumped awake at the sound of her cell phone ringing. Groggy, she grabbed it off of the table next to her and saw that it was Kent. She flipped it open. "Hello?"

Kent cleared his throat. "Babe, it's me."

She frowned and sat up. "What is it?"

"I'm in Birmingham."

"Birmingham?" she said, turning on the lamp. Emily, lying next to her, stirred awake and squinted up at her. "Kent, what are you doing there?"

"It's a long story. But let me talk to Lance."

"Okay." She lowered the phone and looked at the empty bed next to them. "Where's Lance?" she asked Emily.

Emily shook her head. "I don't know."

Barbara got out of bed and threw open the door. Lance wasn't in the hotel hallway. She ran to the banister that overlooked the lobby. "Lance!" she called, not caring who she woke up. But he wasn't there.

"Kent, he's gone!"

Kent muttered something she couldn't hear.

"What's going on?" she shouted. "Tell me!"

There was a pause, then Kent spoke. "We found Carter dead. Let me talk to Emily, and you call Lance from the landline. Get him back there."

Terrified, Barbara went back into the room, put her cell on speakerphone, and thrust the phone at Emily. "Lance is gone. Carter Price is dead."

"What?" Emily took the phone. "Kent, what happened?"

"It's Jack Tyson from Haven House," he said. "He's the one doing this."

Emily froze and looked up at Barbara.

"*Jack?* His last name is Tyson?"

"Who is he?" Barbara asked as she tried to call Lance.

"He got kicked out . . ." Emily's voice trailed off. "Kent, Lance might be with him right now."

Barbara listened as Lance's phone rang through to voice mail. "He's not answering."

Kent grunted. "He was in the hall when I left two hours ago. I told him to go back in."

"He did come in," Emily said, "but he told me he was upset about Tyson being at April's. He went back out to talk on the phone so he wouldn't wake up mom. He might have gone over there."

"Barbara, find Lance. Keep calling him. I'm calling Andy, but you get him home!"

When he hung up, Barbara redialed. Again, it went to voice mail. "Lance Covington," she yelled. "If you're with Jack Tyson, get away from him now and call me! He's the one who killed those women and set fire to Kent's house . . ." Her voice broke. "Oh, Lance, please call me and let me know you're all right!"

She hung up, ready to implode.

"I'll text him," Emily said. "Maybe he's not answering because he's afraid he'll get in trouble for sneaking off."

"Yes," Barbara said, wiping her tears. "Do that."

She waited as Emily texted Lance. As they waited for an answer, Barbara searched the hotel phone book for April's parents, dialed the number.

Her mother answered. "Hello?"

"Mrs. Nelson . . . I don't know your first name, I'm sorry. I'm Barbara, Lance's mother."

"Yes," she said. "I'm Nan."

"Nan, is Lance there with April? I need to talk to him."

"Hold on." She heard sheets rustling, and there was a long pause. Lance still hadn't texted back, but Barbara braced herself, praying he would come to the phone.

Finally, Nan came back. "Barbara, he's not here. I just got home a little while ago and April wasn't here. She didn't leave a note."

"Is my car there?"

"No. Maybe she's out with Lance."

"Nan, do you know if she's seen a guy named Tyson tonight?"

"Probably. I know he was trying to get her to go out with him tonight, but she told me she didn't want to. I guess he could have changed her mind. I was a little distracted at the time, so I'm not sure."

Barbara bit back the urge to tell the woman that she'd better get in the game, because her daughter was probably with a killer.

Trying to calm her voice, she said, "Nan, try to reach your daughter. Her life could be in danger."

When she hung up, Emily shook her head. "Mom, he still hasn't texted."

"Where is he?" Barbara shouted.

Emily crutched across the floor in her pajamas, clutching her phone so she wouldn't miss Lance's text. But nothing came. "I knew this guy Lance kept talking about was bad news. I told him to stay away from him."

"Emily, why didn't you put this together?"

"Because I didn't call him Tyson. I only called him Jack. His last name was on a file somewhere, but if I ever saw it, I don't remember. But Jack knew how close I was to Lance. He's targeting him to hurt me. All this stuff with April. It's not about her at all. It's about Lance. It's about *me!*"

Barbara called Kent back, put him on speakerphone. "Can you trace where his cell phone is? Can you find him, Kent?"

"I'm working on it. Emily, any way you

can get this guy's cell phone number?"

She thought of Lance's other friends. There weren't many. But some of her college classmates were graduates of that high school. Maybe someone knew Tyson. "I'll make some calls."

"Good. Hurry! I'm headed home, and Andy's putting an APB out on Tyson's car. We're running data on him to see what we can find out. Keep calling Lance. I'll be there as soon as I can."

CHAPTER 49

As Kent raced back from Birmingham, blue lights flashing in the grill of his unmarked car and his siren wailing, his shoulder ached where he'd been shot months ago. Fatigue and lack of sleep never did it any good, and the stress of knowing Lance was with the killer made it even worse.

He'd left Bo with the Birmingham police to answer questions about Carter and Tyson, and now he burned up I-20, taking his speed to the top of his car's capability. There was no time to waste. Fortunately there weren't many cars on the road this time of night.

He'd already had Andy send units to Tyson's house to pick him up. But as Kent had suspected, he wasn't home.

He called Andy again. "Where are we?" he asked.

Andy's words came in rapid fire. "We're still trying to track down his car. Nothing

316

yet. But I have Jack Tyson's rap sheet. Several drug charges. Last incarceration was just a few weeks ago. He went to jail in April after violating probation. Was in for four months."

"That was because Emily turned him in. What kind of car is he in?"

"2000 Maxima, black four-door, tag XLB-321. But if he was at your house and later at this girl April's house, when could he have killed Carter?"

"Could have killed him earlier. The body was cold, but I didn't have time to wait for the medical examiner."

"Couple more things on the rap sheet," Andy said. "Went to juvie for two arson charges, one at twelve and again at fourteen. So the whole arson thing, it's not without precedent."

"Anything else?"

"Yeah, actually. The guy is diagnosed with bipolar schizoaffective disorder."

Kent winced. He was no shrink, but he knew that bipolar schizoaffective disorder was much worse than bipolar alone. It was characterized by psychosis, hallucinations, paranoia, and delusions of grandeur, in addition to mania and depression. "So he could suffer from psychosis and delusions. He probably uses drugs to medicate his

317

symptoms, but when he's using, his illness would escalate."

So if Emily was the cause of his having to return to jail, and Tyson had psychotic delusions from his chemical imbalance and paranoia from the drugs, he might have built that "betrayal" up in his mind. And if he'd overheard Bo's and Carter's conversation about murdering each other's wives, he might have seized the opportunity to turn the rehab talk into reality. The power he would feel at making all these things happen would feed into his sense of grandiosity.

But why now? He'd been out of jail for several weeks. Why had it all begun *this* week?

Kent made it back to Atlanta in record time and hurried to the hotel where Barbara and Emily waited. Barbara was a wreck, as he'd expected. She'd dressed, and now she paced in the hotel room, that same look of determination on her face that she'd worn when he'd first met her.

"Kent, we have to go look for them," she cried. "Lance is in danger. He's trying to protect April, but Tyson will kill him. Lance doesn't even know Tyson is the one."

"Every cop on shift right now is looking." Kent went to Emily who sat on the bed, talking on the phone. When she got off, she said, "I got Tyson's cell phone number!"

Barbara looked at her. "How did you do that?"

"I called a guy I know from AA who went to Lance's school last year. He used to buy dope from Tyson."

"Great," Kent said. "I want you to text Tyson. Tell him you're craving. Ask if he can hook you up."

Emily's eyebrows lifted. "He won't believe that. He'll know I'm looking for Lance."

"But he's delusional," Kent said. "And if it's you he's trying to hurt, Lance is just a tool for him anyway. Make it look like he can get right to you if he wants you. If he texts you back, tell him you want him to come pick you up."

"Kent, I don't want her going anywhere with him!" Barbara shouted.

"She's not going to meet him," Kent said. "We're just baiting him."

Barbara seemed to hold her breath as Emily texted Tyson:

Tyson, this is Emily Covington. I'm really jonesing for crack 2nite. Can u hook me up?

They waited, watching the phone, each praying silently. In a few minutes, her phone chimed.

"What does he say?" Barbara demanded.

Emily read. *Well well. The lovely Emily needs my help?* She looked at Kent with dull eyes. "Jerk."

"Okay, ask him if Lance is with him. Ask him to come get you, too."

She typed:

I know my brother's with u. Can u come get me 2?

After a moment, he texted back.

Busy now. Lance about 2 fly.

Barbara grabbed the dresser, almost fell. "What is he doing?"

Kent stood up and steadied her. "He's just trying to yank Emily's chain. That's the whole purpose of his relationship with Lance and April. Emily, tell him it has to be now."

Emily texted:

Can't wait till morning. Come on I have a hundred bucks.

This time there was no answer. They all stood frozen, staring at the phone.

"I'm gonna be sick," Barbara whispered.

Kent had Andy check out Tyson's cell phone service and found out what tower he'd pinged on those last texts. He was somewhere near Decatur, within a fifteen-mile radius of that cell tower. At least they knew he was still in the Atlanta area.

CHAPTER 50

Tyson sped down Howard Avenue at ninety in a fifty-mile-per-hour zone, windows rolled down and his hair blowing in the wind, heavy metal music pounding in his ears. In one hand he clutched the .44 magnum that had gotten April into his car.

But she was a buzzkill. She sulked and cried, trying to make him give her the gun and return her phone. But he couldn't do that. She'd done what he wanted — called Lance to come rescue her. Moron that she was, she still didn't realize that she was just a pawn in a game . . . just a way to get to Lance, who was a way to torture Emily.

It had all been too easy. Tyson had forced April into his car and told her to call Lance to come to her rescue. Her cryptic, desperate call about the tower was sure to draw him out. Lance was probably on his way there.

Just where Tyson wanted him.

It was just too fun. One by one he'd dismantled their lives. He was in control, setting things right. Carter's death had thrilled him.

Lance's would be even more fun, because it would twist the knife in Emily. Then he'd take care of her last.

He reached the intersection where the Decatur water tower stood, that landmark where his father's life had changed and his family's slow death had begun. What had paralyzed his father was now his own stage.

"Please take me home," April cried. "You're scaring me."

"Not till you climb with me," he said. "I want you to see the lights. Feel the wind and the cold from up above the ground. Get high up there in the sky."

He loved her terror.

He pulled over the curb with a bump and rolled as close as he could to the chain-link fence. Clutching his gun with his left hand, he made April hold the pipe and filled it with his right. Her hand shook so bad that she couldn't hold it still, but he managed to light a flame under it. He took a long, deep hit, then thrust it back at her. "Come on, baby. It'll make you feel better."

"No," she sobbed. "Tyson, I won't tell

anybody about the gun. Please . . . just let me go."

He felt the rush working through his brain cells, igniting his neurons. "No, baby, you're gonna climb. Come on, you'll love it."

"You could fall like your dad."

"No, I don't fall," he assured her. "I never fall. I fly, baby."

He used the gun to force her out of the car. She was trembling head to toe, wind tossing her hair. He made her climb the four-foot fence, and he followed, anxious to reach the top.

Lance saw Tyson's car when he reached Paden Circle. He turned the corner, went over the curb onto the grass.

Then he saw them, climbing the tower.

He groped for his phone. As it lit up, he saw that he'd had several calls and texts from Emily and his mother. He'd forgotten the phone was on silence.

No time to call them back now. He had to call the police.

The 911 operator answered.

"There's a guy holding a girl hostage at the Decatur water tower!" he blurted.

"Is he armed?"

"I don't know," he said. "But please . . . hurry. He could kill her."

He cut off the phone just as he heard April's scream. Leaving the phone on his console, he bolted out of the car.

Tyson saw the headlights illuminating them. Lance had come.

Perfect.

A car door slammed. "Tyson!" Lance yelled.

Tyson had almost gotten her to the top. "Go over the rail, onto the catwalk," he ordered.

Whining and blubbering, she froze.

Tyson glanced back. Lance had jumped the fence and was coming toward the ladder.

"He's got a gun!" April screamed.

Lance didn't back down. He came closer, as if he thought he could disarm Tyson by sheer will. "Drop the gun, Tyson!" he called up.

"Climb, April!" Tyson said, jabbing her leg with the gun.

Lance started climbing. "Tyson, I called the police when I got here . . . they'll be here any minute."

"Perfect," Tyson said. "The bigger the audience, the better. Nobody stops me. Not my mother, who's been laying in bed in her own blood for four days . . . and surely not

324

the police."

He summoned all the strength of the drugs pulsing through him to get himself and April onto the catwalk.

As Lance climbed the tower's ladder, he heard April crying. "April, the police are coming," he called. "Just do what he says."

"The police can't help you, precious," Tyson said to April, then called down to Lance, "and big sis can't help you either, Lancelot. She talked about you all the time. About how the worst thing that could happen would be if you followed in her footsteps, got into drugs, ruined your life like she did."

Sweat dripped into Lance's eyes. "How do you even know her?"

"She worked at Haven House. High and mighty, got me thrown in jail."

Lance froze on the ladder, trying to make sense of what Tyson had said. Then it came to him. Tyson . . . he'd committed all these crimes. *He* had killed those women, bombed Emily's car, set fire to Kent's house . . . "All this . . . is about her? *You're* the one?"

Tyson laughed like a demon in a burning church.

Now more than ever, Lance wanted to reach Tyson and put an end to all this. But

Tyson was insane. He might push April off the tower without a thought.

Lance tried to distract him. "You killed your mother?" he asked. "Is she really dead in her bed?"

"Yeah, I killed her," Tyson said through his teeth. "She nagged me, she tortured my dad — I put him out of his misery, too. Now I'm free. I'm the Avenger!" He raised his arms and screamed out a victory shout.

Nausea swept over Lance, but he fought it back. Where were the police?

April sobbed, gulping wind. Lance pulled himself up, his breath coming harder, his lungs unable to keep up. He thought of Tyson shooting his mother, leaving her in her bed for days.

God, please get the police here!

Tyson's cell phone chimed with a text. Emily again? He came out of his victory stance, pulled his phone out of his pocket.

Tyson, I'm really jonesing for crack 2night. Can u hook me up?

He laughed. She must know that he had Lance.

Or maybe she really did want a hit. Her sober act was destined to fail. The drugs had a stronger pull than any decision she could make.

His mind raced in a million directions as he watched Lance climbing higher. April sat on the catwalk, legs bent, arms hugging her knees. He thought of Emily, craving and crawling, of his father locked in that wheelchair, of his mother lying in the bed where he'd leveled things with her four days ago. The freedom her death had given him had opened the floodgates, allowing him to do all that he'd done this week. Allowing him the power to be the great Avenger.

No one had yet found her body, or his father's either, strapped in his wheelchair where he'd been stuck, since his scuffle with this tower. Powerless, sitting in his own waste with his hands strapped down.

"Tyson, please . . ."

April's plea snapped his racing thoughts back. This was the snowcapped mountaintop. The *coup de grâce.* He felt the power rising inside him, threatening to explode through his own skin and break him free of human trappings.

He watched, grinning, as Lance reached the top. The wind picked up, making the fire in his ears and his neck, his fingers and toes, cool a degree. "Over the rail, Lance. Join us, won't you?" Throwing his head back, he wheezed with laughter.

Lance came over the rail. Wind whipped

through his hair. "Here I am, Tyson. Just let her go."

"The only way she's coming off this tower is if I shove her. I love that idea."

Tyson stood between them, blocking Lance's path to April. Whimpering, April slid sideways, trying to get away from Tyson, but there was nowhere she could go. Lance moved closer, but Tyson stopped him by pointing the pistol in his direction.

Only one thing would make this perfect. Emily. Still pointing the weapon at Lance and holding his phone with his left hand, Tyson typed with his thumb:

Sure can, babe. Knew u couldn't hold out much longer.

"Come on, Tyson." Lance's voice was low, gentle.

Emily's reply chimed back.

I know Lance is with u. Can u come get me 2?

Tyson shrieked with laughter. She knew. Was she worried about her brother or her own appetites? Tyson thought of bringing Emily up here with him, shooting her veins full of fuel, watching her fly . . .

But not now. This was too good.

Busy now, he typed. *Lance about 2 fly.*

He hoped that felt like a knife in her chest. But he couldn't tell from her reply: *Come on I have a hundred bucks.*

His mind raced. Her desperation filled him with glee. The need. He loved her need. He thought of all they could do together, just him and her and a syringe. . . . The perfect revenge would be starting her downfall, tangling her up with desperation, just before she went to prison for all the things he'd done.

He started to text her again, but his thumb hit the wrong icon. The screen filled with "CALL," and her number came up, searching for a cell tower, connecting . . .

He started to press END, but suddenly Lance was on him, trying to grab the gun, making him loosen his grip. Tyson dropped the phone as he grabbed the gun with both hands, trying to move the barrel toward Lance's forehead. But Lance grabbed Tyson's wrists and forced his arms up, the barrel pointing toward the sky. The phone bounced once on the steel deck beneath them, then disappeared from his vision. Tyson cursed.

April screamed for help, hollering like a tortured animal. Tyson kicked Lance, knocking him back, then turned to April, the gun cold in his itching fingers.

He raised the barrel and pulled the trigger.

CHAPTER 51

"It's him!" Emily cried. "Tyson's calling!"

Kent lunged toward the phone, but didn't take it. "Answer it on speakerphone and keep him talking. Try to find out where he is."

On the third ring, she took a deep breath, clicked ANSWER, and set the phone on the table. "Hello?"

Nothing but wind, cars passing, the sound of a faint, distant voice.

"Hello? Tyson?"

On his own phone, Kent punched out the department number, hoping they could trace Tyson's call.

"Hello?" Emily said louder. "Tyson?"

There was no answer. She turned up the volume. "Tyson?" she yelled.

"Is it an accidental call?" Barbara asked.

They listened to the voices . . . still faint . . . still distant. Was that a girl screaming . . . crying . . . ?

"Oh, dear God, help us," Barbara whispered.

Kent picked up the phone, took it off speaker, and listened. "I hear a man's voice, but I can't make out what he's saying. He sounds a long way away."

He muted the call, held Emily's phone to one ear, and with the other, brought his own phone to his mouth. "Madge, Kent Harlan. I need a trace of this cell phone number." He read Tyson's number from the screen on Emily's phone. "Can you get a GPS fix on it?"

The air in the hotel room seemed thin, and perspiration coated his face as he waited. Finally, she spoke. "It looks like the phone is at the East Lake MARTA Station, or at least in that area."

"Thanks. Do me a favor and get some units dispatched to that area. And let Andy know this is our guy."

Kent cut the call off. "I'm going there now."

"What if he realizes what's happened and gets on the phone?"

"Then I'll talk to him."

"But he's expecting to talk to me," she said. "Let me go with you. If he gets back on the phone, I can talk to him."

Kent hesitated, looking at Barbara.

"Whatever we do, we have to hurry!" she cried. "He's going to kill them! Come on, we'll all go."

Kent heard sirens over the phone line. The police were already approaching! Someone else must have called before him. "All right, come on."

They raced out to his car. Emily got in the backseat. They put Tyson's call back on speakerphone, with the phone muted, as they flew to the area, the blue light in Kent's grill flashing. Kent called Andy and filled him in.

Emily and Barbara listened to Tyson's call, trying to make out the voices and the sounds around them. The sirens had stopped. "It doesn't sound like they're in a train station," Emily told Kent. "It sounds like they're outside."

They heard the girl's distant screaming again, the whoop of celebration.

But they didn't hear Lance.

CHAPTER 52

"Has the phone moved?" Kent yelled into his cell as he flew toward Decatur.

"No," his phone company contact said. "It hasn't moved since we first located it."

"Let me know if it moves one inch." He glanced at Emily in his rearview mirror. "Anything changed?"

"No. We can still hear a girl screaming," Barbara said. "Kent, please hurry!"

The radio crackled. ". . . reported disturbance at Howard Avenue and Paden Circle, across from East Lake MARTA . . ."

"That's it!" Barbara cried.

Kent grabbed the mike and radioed the dispatcher to repeat the call.

"Before your call, there was another call about a man holding a woman hostage at the Decatur water tower across from the East Lake MARTA."

"The water tower! That's our suspect,"

Kent said into the radio. "Is he on the tower?"

"We're not sure yet. Units just arrived at the scene."

He heard her transmission to the officer who'd arrived there first. Static again, then: "There are three people on the tower."

"Lance is up there!" Barbara shouted. "God, please!"

As they approached the MARTA station, Kent saw police cars flashing blue strobes. Mood lights illuminated the water tower with the name Decatur shining in big block letters. There was Barbara's car.

Into his radio, Kent said, "We need some snipers here as fast as you can get them to us. This guy is holding two people hostage, and we have to assume he's armed. And get this highway blocked off." He slowed at the MARTA station. "Get out, both of you. Wait at the train station. I can't take you there with me."

Barbara and Emily didn't argue. They jumped out, both looking across the lanes of traffic at the tower.

"Go inside," he said. "Hurry."

When they headed inside, he crossed the lanes of traffic and pulled up to the tower. He left his headlights on, adding to the others shining on the tower.

Victorious whoops echoed down as Tyson leaned against the rail, arms raised. Suddenly there was a gunshot.

Kent dropped to the ground behind his car door, straining to see if Lance was still standing.

CHAPTER 53

Lance wished he knew how many bullets Tyson had had in his chamber when he'd started shooting. So far he'd shot three times, and he was getting crazier. The spotlights the police shone on them blinded them, but the blue lights below gave Lance some hope. Maybe they could stop Tyson, force him to let them down.

Tyson jumped from foot to foot like a boxer in the ring. He'd probably gone days without sleep — ever since he'd murdered his parents — and now the drugs and the delusion mingled in a frightening brand of insanity.

But Lance's mind was clear. If he could just think . . . be smart. Play into Tyson's delusions.

"We're on TV, baby," Tyson said. "Those are spotlights. They're filming me. I'm a star."

"You'll be famous," Lance agreed. "The

guy who scaled the tower. The guy who conquered it."

"Got that right!" Tyson shouted, then whooped again. "I could fly. Wouldn't they love that, on live television? If I stepped up here on the rail and spread out my wings, and just launched myself on the wind?"

Lance thought of bringing him back to reality, telling him that he didn't *have* wings, but Tyson's delusions might be their only hope. Lance's mouth was dry. "You could get your own reality show. You'd have fans all over the world."

A red dot appeared on Tyson's chest, moving around in a tiny circle. A light like a laser . . .

Lance looked at the police cars clustered below them, but couldn't see the origin of the red light, cutting in a straight line through the blinding light of the spotlight.

He'd seen it in movies. The lasers of high-tech gun sights. They were going to shoot Tyson.

He felt weak, but he had to be strong. He had to move himself and April away from Tyson.

As Tyson leaned on the rail, his arms spread as he screamed a victory whoop. Lance slipped behind him and got between Tyson and April.

He took a step to the side, another, putting two feet between them, three feet, pushing April to move away . . . slowly, so Tyson wouldn't react.

Suddenly, Tyson noticed the light on his chest. He tried to sweep it away like a bug. Then his face changed as he realized what it was. He let out an enraged scream that sounded like a tortured vulture.

He lunged toward Lance, grabbed him, and jerked him in front of him. "You kill me, you kill him!" he screamed down. "You hear me?"

Lance prayed that they would hear him, that they could see clearly, that no rookie cop, in the excitement of the moment, would make a mistake. He heard a bullhorn and a familiar voice. "Jack Tyson, this is Detective Kent Harlan. Let me come up and talk to you."

Relief and dread deflated Lance.

"No need!" Tyson screamed down. "He's coming down to *you!*" He shoved Lance, but Lance gasped and caught himself on the rail.

And then he saw the red dot, dancing around on his own chest now. Tyson pushed Lance against the rail, crowding him from behind, his breath hot on the back of Lance's neck. "We're on TV, baby," Tyson said into his ear. "I can let you fly first. Right over the edge. And then I'll be right behind you."

"No, Tyson," Lance said. "I can't fly. I don't have what you have. I'll hit the ground like your father."

"That's how it's supposed to be," Tyson whispered into his ear. "Everything is perfect. Emily will see it all on TV."

"I don't know what she did to you," Lance said, his voice wobbling. "But you've shown her. You have. You've really gotten the best of her."

Tyson shoved him harder against the rail, the gun barrel pressed into his back. Was he going to push him over? That red spot moved up Lance's chest. He couldn't see it anymore. Was it at his throat? His forehead? Were they going to kill them both?

Lance had to do something fast. "I wanted to see you fly," he said, forcing strength into his voice. "I wanted to watch you catch the air. I know you could do it."

"Oh, I could do it," Tyson said, his voice rippling with excitement. "I could catch the air, and it would lift me up, and I'd soar through the air like Superman. I wouldn't fall because gravity has no hold on me."

"If you throw me over," Lance said, "gravity wins. You can't let gravity win."

The logic of his words made Tyson hesitate. "I have to show them that I beat it. I have to show them while they're taping."

"You're on TV, man," Lance said carefully. "They want a show. Either they win or you do."

Tyson let him go, whooped again, and stepped up onto the lower rail. His knees leaned against the top one, and he held out his hands in another victory shout.

"I can fly!" he screamed. "I can defy!"

And then he stepped up to the top rail, spread his arms like wings, and took flight.

CHAPTER 54

As Tyson plunged to the ground, April screamed. She sat on the catwalk, face buried against her knees. Lance fell to her side and put his arms around her, holding her with all his strength.

On the bullhorn, Kent said, "Stay there, Lance. We're coming up to get you." Squinting, Lance saw Kent crossing the fence, running toward the ladder.

In the blinding light he saw a fire truck moving closer, its ladder sliding up toward them. He wanted to stand, but April was limp, so he waited at her side.

When the fire truck's ladder was almost up to them, Kent reached the catwalk, winded from the climb, and came toward them. "Lance, April, don't move," he said.

Lance waited, frozen. When Kent reached them, he helped coax April to her feet. Lance held her as rescuers surrounded her and got her onto the fire truck's ladder.

As Lance got on behind her, he heard his mother's voice some distance away. He looked toward the MARTA station and saw her and Emily running across the highway. When he reached the ground, she almost crushed him as she threw her arms around him, weeping and thanking God aloud. Over her shoulder, Lance watched April. Shivering, she was staring at the body on the ground. Tyson lay face-down, lifeless.

Gravity had won.

Paramedics crowded around him . . . but there was no hurry. Tyson was dead. The nightmare was over.

CHAPTER 55

Kent went with Andy and Strand to Tyson's house, where they found his mother dead in her bed and his father lifeless in his wheel-chair, just as Tyson had bragged.

The three of them interviewed neighbors who knew the family well. From what Kent heard from them about the constant abuse Tyson had experienced from his mother and the trauma of his father's helplessness, along with his constant drug use, it was clear that he must have had a mental breakdown that led to his mother's murder first. Then, out of a twisted sense of compassion, he'd killed his father. The two murders had unleashed the streak of revenge for every wrong done to him, beginning with the three who'd angered him in rehab. When they found a list of people in his room — with Emily, Bo, and Carter at the top — they knew that his murderous spree would have gone on and on if he had not been stopped.

From his cell phone and notes in his room, they were able to get the numbers of most of his drug suppliers. They turned those over to the Department of Narcotics.

Now, back at his office, Kent pulled the ring out of his pocket and turned it in the light.

Andy came up behind him. "So when are you gonna do it, man?"

Kent grinned. "Soon. But I want to talk to the kids first."

"Hey, it's her life, not theirs."

"It's theirs, too," Kent said. "It matters what they think. If they want me to wait, well . . ."

Andy chuckled. "Well, what?"

Kent thought that over. What would he do? Call the whole thing off? "Well, I'll just have to cry and beg."

Andy clearly enjoyed picturing that.

Monday afternoon, Kent went to Lance's school. He parked across the street just as the day's last bell rang. He strolled up the carpool line of cars, looking for Barbara's car, which Emily was still driving. He found it idling halfway up the line. Going to the passenger side, he knocked on her window. She looked up from the textbook she was reading and popped her lock. "Hey!" she said as he opened the door. "Didn't expect to see you."

"Mind if I get in?" he asked.

"Sure," she said, handing him the crutches in her passenger seat. "You can put these in the back."

He moved the crutches, then slid into the seat. "I wanted to tell you that the charges against you are dropped. You're free and clear."

She leaned back on the seat, breathing relief. "Thank goodness."

"How did it go with your test?"

"Dr. Ingles let me make it up today. I'm hoping for a good grade."

"You'll be fine." He hesitated, suddenly nervous. "Listen, I want to talk to you and Lance about something else."

"Okay. About what?"

"About your mom."

A slow smile made its way across her face. "Oh. Got it."

He grinned and looked out the window, saw Lance coming out in a flood of students. A girl was shoving him, laughing and flirting. Some other guys were following Lance as if he was the conquering hero. He'd been all over the news this morning, interviewed about risking his life to save April. Her own interview confirmed his heroism, and one of the channels had replayed Missouri footage of his heroism a year ago, as well.

Emily smiled as she watched her brother through the windshield. "Things are looking up for Lance."

"Guess he's not the class pariah anymore. That's good."

Lance spent a few minutes talking to the friends clustered around him. He was in a great mood when he got in, and they headed off to the Dairy Queen around the corner from the school. Other kids were there when they arrived, and they high-fived Lance and patted his back as he ordered.

Kent watched him with pride, like a proud father. When he got his food, Lance slid into their booth. Keeping his voice low, he said, "So at lunch today, April asked if I'd take her to homecoming."

"Way to go," Emily said. "Did you say yes?"

Lance shrugged and studied his fries. "Not yet. I told her that I didn't want to hang out with her if she was even thinking about doing dope again. She says she's learned her lesson, that she never wants to mess with anybody who does drugs. Took almost dying to realize that dopers have their own special flavor of insanity."

"Wasn't that enough for you?" Kent asked.

Lance shrugged. "I don't know. I'll probably go with her. But this other girl asked me. Pink Paget."

"Pink?" Emily asked. "Her name is *Pink,* and she's not a rock star?"

"Yeah, but listen."

"Her mother named her that?" Emily said, incredulous. "It's on her birth certificate?"

"How do I know what's on her birth certificate? But she asked me if I'd show her my scar, so I unbuttoned my shirt and
—"

Kent winced. "Lance, you didn't."

"Why not? I showed her the scar over my lung, and before I knew it there was a crowd. Everybody wanted to see."

"No way."

"Way. It was great. All this time those jocks were calling me a liar, and now they believe everything. Then Pink asked for my phone number and she asked me to homecoming. And she's in the youth group on-fire-for-Jesus crowd, so I don't see her smoking dope the next time somebody offers her a joint."

"Hey, church kids can go off the rails, too," Emily said.

"I know, but still . . ."

"It's always good to have options," Kent said. "I knew you'd be the big man on campus before you knew what hit you."

Emily shoved a spoonful of ice cream into her mouth. "Almost worth a near-death experience, huh?"

"Not really." Lance sobered, leaning back. "April's traumatized. Her mom is putting her into counseling. I think that's a good thing. She needs help with her issues, not drugs. And her parents need to get their act together."

Finally, Emily asked Kent the obvious. "So what did you want to talk to us about?"

Kent's laughter faded and nerves took over. He cleared his throat, folded his hands in front of his face. "You guys know how crazy I am about your mother."

Emily smiled. "Feeling seems to be mutual."

"Good." He leaned forward, crossed his hands in front of him. "Because I want to ask her to marry me."

The kids were silent for a moment, and he couldn't read their faces. Had he made a mistake? Were they unhappy about it? Finally, Lance broke into a grin. "Well, it's about time."

Relief almost made him go limp. "Really? You've been expecting this? Do you think she'll say yes?"

"We didn't move here for nothing," Emily said. "But are you sure it's not just because

348

you need a place to live?"

For a moment he thought she was serious, then she burst out laughing. "The house can be fixed," he said. "I have a construction crew there already." He stared into Emily's amused face. "Are you okay with this, Emily?"

Her smile faded, but it still sparkled in her eyes. She set her spoon down and leaned on the table, her gaze locking with his. "I miss my dad a lot. I wish things could be like they used to be, but they can't. You already feel like part of the family. Let's just make it official."

His throat tightened. "Thank you, Emily. And Lance?"

Lance couldn't hide his grin. "Hey, man, I'm in. Our family needs constant police protection."

Laughing, Kent reached into his pocket and pulled out the ring he'd been carrying for way too long. "What do you think?"

Emily sucked in a breath. "Gorgeous!"

Lance laughed and fist-bumped him. "Did good, dude. So how are you gonna ask her? It's gotta be something good."

"Then help me figure out something. What should I do?"

"Hot air balloons!" Emily said. "You take her up in a hot air balloon and ask her up in the sky."

"Yeah, and don't let her out until she says yes."

Kent laughed. "Where would I find a hot air balloon? Besides, your mom doesn't need any more stress. I want it to be something nice and calm."

"That's true," Emily said. "Matter of fact, she's probably not going to want to plan a wedding. The last thing she needs is another situation where she's in charge of details."

"Hey, I know," Lance said. "You could take her to a ball game and put it on the scoreboard."

"That's been done a zillion times," Emily said. "How about this? You take her on a nostalgia tour."

"A what?"

"A tour through your past together. Like where you first met, where your first date was . . ."

"Um, I met her at a murder scene, in the garage of the Atlanta airport. I don't think she'd enjoy that stroll down memory lane."

"True," Emily said. "Bad idea."

They were all quiet for a moment as they racked their brains. "Have you thought of dinner at a fancy restaurant?" Lance asked. "Just the two of you. You do the whole getting-down-on-one-knee thing? It's bor-

ing and all, but Mom likes boring sometimes."

"That's cliché," Emily said. "You want to
do something different. You need a great
story."

"You're confusing me," Kent said.

"Just ask her, man," Lance said. "Mom
will like things low-key, like Emily said.
She's been living in high drama for the last
few days. And they just got the job building
the church sanctuary, so she's overloaded.
Stress-free is what she'll like."

"So you think she'll say yes?"

"Oh, she'll say yes," Emily assured him.

He was silent for a moment as he regarded
both of them. "Then I think I know what
would work. But I'll need help from both of
you."

CHAPTER 56

The line to get the new car tags was mercifully short that Friday. Barbara hoped she could be out of there and back at work in the time she would have taken for lunch. She waited as someone who didn't speak English tried to communicate with a clerk. Barbara fixed her gaze on the window of another clerk, who was almost finished with the man she was waiting on.

The insurance company had decided to total Emily's car. Instead of just replacing it, Barbara used the insurance money for down payments on two used cars — one for Emily and one for Lance. A church friend who worked at a dealership had quickly found her two old cars in good condition, and if they could keep them running, it would make all of their lives easier.

She'd been conflicted about the whole thing — whether to ground Lance for life for sneaking out and rushing into danger, or to reward him for putting April's life before his own. Her pride in his heroism trumped her maternal anger. So Lance was getting the car for which they'd been saving.

She got to the window, paid for the tags, and waited as the clerk typed the information about both cars into her computer. Finally, Barbara took the tags, stuffed them into her bag, and stepped out of the office.

She caught her breath when she saw Kent, dressed in a tuxedo, a soft smile on his face.

"Kent, what are you doing?"

"I was hoping I'd catch you here," he said.

She could see the mischief in his twinkling eye. He took her hand.

"Kent? What is it? Why are you so dressed up?"

He walked her a few steps up the hall. "I thought while you were here, you might want to stop by this office." He turned her to the door that said MARRIAGE LICENSES.

Her heart jolted, and she brought her hand to her mouth.

He pulled her inside the county clerk's office, and before she could speak, knelt on one knee, holding a sparkling diamond ring in a little black velvet box. His eyes misted. "Barbara, I don't want to wait another day to start my life with you."

Tears filled her eyes, and she bent to frame his face with her hands. "I don't either," she whispered.

"Will you marry me?"

She kissed him as he came to his feet. "Yes! Yes, I'll marry you!"

"Now?" he said.

Only then did she realize that the woman behind the desk was videotaping them. She laughed and wiped her tears. "What do you mean *now?*"

"I mean now. We can get the license here. There's no waiting period, no blood test, no nothing. We can get married today."

She stared at him, then looked at the grinning stranger with the camcorder. Married today? But she didn't have a dress. She'd thrown on a pair of pants and a blouse today, she hardly had any makeup on, and her hair was a mess.

Was this how she wanted to marry Kent?

Suddenly, joy erupted in her heart and spread across her face. "Okay, let's do it."

The office staff applauded. Barbara was giddy as they filled out their marriage license application, then waited until they were given the form in a white envelope.

"Good luck," the woman said, handing Kent the camcorder.

Kent stopped before taking Barbara out

and kissed her in the doorway. Were they going to do this right here, with a judge? Suddenly she had cold feet. She couldn't marry him *today!* Not without Emily or Lance.

"Mom?"

Barbara spun around.

Beaming, Emily waited in the hallway just outside the door, balancing on her crutches and holding an ivory silk dress and a short veil in her arms. "I think you would have picked this out for yourself."

Barbara gasped and took the dress. "It's perfect! Oh, honey!"

"Then let's go get you married," Emily said.

"And I don't have to *do* anything?"

"Nope," Kent said. "It's all done. The preacher's waiting at the church, and our friends will be arriving soon. You have plenty of time to get ready."

"What about Lance? He's in school."

"I got him out early," Kent said. "You had me on his emergency list, remember? I figured a wedding was a good enough reason. The principal gave him an excused absence."

Teary-eyed, she took the dress so Emily could crutch out. They stepped out of the building, and in front of a limousine stood

Lance, outfitted in his own black tux. He looked so mature, so handsome in it. He, too, was grinning from ear to ear. "Well, did she say yes or what?"

Barbara threw up her hands. "Of course I did!"

Lance let out a whoop as the chauffeur opened the back door. "Then let's go do this!" Barbara felt like royalty as she got into the car with the people she loved most in her life, and headed off for the church.

CHAPTER 57

Barbara changed into her wedding dress in the bride's room at the church, marveling at the fact that Emily had found an ivory calf-length dress that was perfect for the occasion. Emily had also brought her shoes, makeup, curling iron, and hair spray. Barbara hurried to get ready, and Emily fussed around her, helping her to look bridal. When she finally felt ready and put the shoulder-length veil on, she went to the atrium and found Kent waiting.

The misty emotion in his eyes moved her as he kissed her and took her hand. Lance handed her the bouquet he was holding — white roses. "So here's how it's gonna be, Mom. Emily will go first, then me, and then when the *Wedding March* starts, Kent is gonna escort you in himself. We thought you'd like that."

"That's just fine."

"Okay." Lance cracked the door open, and

nodded to someone. The organist wrapped up the song she was playing, and changed to Pachelbel's *Canon in D.*

As the doors opened, Barbara caught a glimpse of the people who had come for them. Cousins from out of town, the ladies from her support group in Jeff City, church friends, and co-workers. Emily led the march, her crutches decorated with roses and ribbons. Lance followed.

She hoped the makeup she'd put on would stand up to her tears. "You did all this for me!" she whispered to Kent as she took his arm.

"It's not too much too fast, is it?" he asked.

"It's perfect in every way. No stress, no details, no plans. Just happily ever after."

Smiling through tears, Barbara started down the aisle with Kent. Friends old and new beamed at them, celebrating their vows as the preacher led them over the threshold of marriage.

When the vows had been exchanged, Barbara and Kent knelt at the altar and prayed for blessings on their covenant.

When they rose to their feet again, they each kissed Emily, then Lance. Then the preacher said the words they'd been waiting for. "I now pronounce you husband and wife."

The crowd burst into applause as Kent kissed his bride.

Barbara, Kent, Emily, and Lance dined at the top of the Peachtree Westin that night to celebrate the nuptials. They talked jubilantly, enjoying the moment of peace and the new beginning they were embarking on.

Then, when they were finished, Emily and Lance hugged them good-bye, and Barbara and Kent spent a night in the honeymoon suite at the Four Seasons.

"This is a dream come true for me, Mrs. Harlan," Kent said as he held his bride. "When I met you two years ago, I never dreamed I could even be in your league."

She laughed. "My league? I feel like the plain Jane who got a date with the quarterback. Let's face it," she said. "We both did well. And to think we met at a murder scene, during one of the worst days of my life."

"Just goes to show you. Even when it seems like the end, God can plant a beginning."

"I like beginnings," she whispered.

They celebrated their first night as true husband and wife, then lay in bed watching a laugh-a-thon on one of the cable stations, with one romantic comedy after another.

Barbara realized she could get used to this. Already, she felt their lives shifting, things changing. The years of darkness were behind them, and a bright new day had dawned. Beauty had indeed come from the garbage of their lives. Darkness had brought light. Despair gave way to joy.

God's grace overrode it all. No matter what lay ahead, joy was a done deal.

A NOTE FROM THE AUTHOR

A few years ago when I started writing the Intervention Series, I had come through a long journey with my daughter who had addictions. My portrayal of Barbara, the mother in this series, was inspired by my own experiences and emotions as I tried to help my daughter.

Since that time, I've met or heard from many of you who are experiencing the same thing. Drug abuse is a cancer eating its way across our world, and it's destroying generations. So many of you are heartbroken because you can't save your loved ones. Believe me, I understand.

Recently, while walking through a valley myself, I discovered an audio series called Faith in the Night Seasons, by Nancy Missler. I've been listening to the audio sessions and have found that they minister to me in a wonderful way. I don't know her, but I thought the series was so powerful that

I wanted you to have a chance to buy it. You can find it at www.khouse.org. Type "Faith in the Night Seasons" into the search box, and you'll see the various products associated with it.

In this series, Nancy Missler talks about a terrible night season she endured when her husband's business went bankrupt, her house and earthly belongings were destroyed in an earthquake, and her thirty-nine-year-old son died of a heart attack while he was out jogging. All of this happened within a two-year period. She talks about the feeling that God had abandoned her, or that he was punishing her for some reason. Her son's sudden death was a burden that crushed her, and no matter how hard she tried, she could not come to any understanding of it, and God offered no explanation.

But now, having come through that dark night, she sees the ways God used it. Her own mother came to Christ because of her son's death. Others were influenced and changed. And the dark night that influenced her to write the books and tapes in this series have certainly ministered to me, and hopefully will to you.

That's all very nice, but when it's you in the dark night, when you're in the depths of your pain, hope is a distant flicker. But the point of my writing the Intervention Series, and the point of Nancy Missler's series, is to tell you that in those times, we can't trust our emotions or our circumstances. We have to remember what we know about Christ and His promises — not what we feel. We may feel abandoned and lonely and devastated. We may cry out for answers. We may demand to know the purpose. Sometimes, it just isn't given.

In those times, our faith is tested more than ever. Some turn away from God. Others grow closer, more dependent on Him. Nancy Missler says, "Pure faith is accepting those situations in your life that you cannot fully understand, and no longer being troubled by them."

Wow. That is faith. If we can see our trials from a heavenly perspective and trust that God has a purpose even when we can't see it, then it is truly possible to enter that dark night of the soul when God seems to be silent . . . and trust Him anyway. It is possible to accept the trials that come into our lives and not be troubled by them.

Possible, but not easy. It takes spiritual maturity, intimate prayer, and a constant feeding on God's Word. When I'm in a dark night, I don't feel hungry for God's Word.

But if I had no appetite for food, I'd still understand that I needed it to survive. I need God's Word in order to survive my trials, whether I feel like reading it or not.

I'd love to tell you I'm at that place where I'm no longer troubled by my trials. That is the case with some of my trials — some of those that seem unaddressed by God. But others still plague me, and I grapple my way through the dark of those nights, still crying out to God for help and explanations and resolution.

One day, I hope I'll come to that place where my faith is strong enough to trust God completely, and no longer be troubled by suffering. It's something we can all work on.

But whatever state I'm in, whether I'm walking through a dark night or enjoying the bright light of day, I know this for certain: "As for me, I know that my Redeemer lives, and at the last He will take His stand on the earth" (Job 19:25). All things will be made new, and there will be no more pain. He will dry every tear, and right every wrong.

Come quickly, Lord Jesus!
Terri Blackstock

QUESTIONS FOR DISCUSSION

1. Once problems start arising, Barbara fears her daughter is getting into trouble with drugs again. Emily insists she's not. Do you think Barbara is justified in her fears? Or do you think she should trust Emily more?

2. Emily has recovered from an addiction and from her past wrong choices, but the effects of those choices seem to follow her into the future. Do you think someone with such a littered past can really move on with his or her life?

3. When Emily is in jail, she says to her cellmate, "I guess it doesn't really matter what we were before . . . what matters is what we are now. We're supposed to move forward from wherever we are, and not look back." What do you think about this idea of moving forward and not looking back? To what extent do we need to look back to make sure we aren't making the

same mistakes?

4. Emily looks at her situation as similar to that of Joseph's in the Bible. She trusts that God will work out her circumstances for the good, as he did with Joseph and his brothers. Have you ever been in a situation where you felt like Joseph? How did God carry you through that situation?

5. Emily's brother, Lance, struggles with many things: adjusting to an unfamiliar community, being an outcast at school, and going along for the ride while his sister faces one crisis after another. How does Lance avoid falling into the same destructive patterns that his sister did?

6. When Tyson, April, and Lance first go to the water tower, there is a moment when Tyson seems to show a bit of his past and his hurt. Despite Tyson's obvious problems, do you think he has any good qualities? Where did things go wrong?

7. Emily goes to Scripture when she's feeling fearful and discouraged. She reads in Numbers 14:9, "Only do not rebel against the Lord. And do not be afraid of the people of the land, because we will swallow them up. Their protection is gone, but the Lord is with us. Do not be afraid of them." What does this verse mean to you?

How did it help Emily through her problems?

8. Emily nearly slips back into her drug addiction. Were you surprised that she was able to walk away from the drugs and stay clean? Why or why not?

9. What do you think of the way Kent proposed? Do you think it was the perfect way to marry Barbara? Why or why not? What do you think their marriage means to them? To Emily and Lance?

10. What has the Intervention Series meant to you? Has it changed your thinking about drug abuse and its challenges? Has it made you more sympathetic to families going through it? Has it given you hope?

The employees of Thorndike Press hope you have enjoyed this Large Print book. All our Thorndike, Wheeler, and Kennebec Large Print titles are designed for easy reading, and all our books are made to last. Other Thorndike Press Large Print books are available at your library, through selected bookstores, or directly from us.

For information about titles, please call:
(800) 223-1244

or visit our Web site at:
http://gale.cengage.com/thorndike

To share your comments, please write:
Publisher
Thorndike Press
10 Water St., Suite 310
Waterville, ME 04901